Lifeblood

By

Werner Lind

World Castle Publishing

Werner Lind

This is a work of fiction. Names, characters, places, and incidents are products of the author's imagination or are used fictitiously and are not to be construed as real. Any resemblance to actual events, locations, organizations, or person, living or dead, is entirely coincidental.

World Castle Publishing
Pensacola, Florida

Copyright © Werner Lind 2004
ISBN: 9781938243646
First Edition Silverlake Publishing February 2004
Second Edition World Castle Publishing June 15, 2012
http://www.worldcastlepublishing.com

Cover: Karen Fuller

Dedication

To my wife Barb
who inspired me, encouraged me, helped me in the creation of this
book, and believed that it had a future even at times when I didn't.
Brown Eyes, I couldn't have done it without you!

Werner Lind

Chapter One

It was a bitter winter night in 1665. In the chill moonlight reflecting off the deep snow, Ana Vasilifata could see each of her own breaths, small vapory clouds, in front of her. Shivering, she drew her high-collared black cloak more tightly around her and glanced up to study the sky. At this small hour, the smoke from the banked fires of thousands of dwellings in the nearby city of London was not sufficient to obscure the positions of the stars. From her scrutiny of the sky, she guessed that sunrise was not far off, perhaps less than an hour away. She leaned for a moment against the dark bole of an ash tree beside the path, permitting herself a brief pause to catch her breath. Cold wind whistled dully around her, stirring the cloak that wrapped her six-foot form.

Reaching up with numb hands, she brushed her loose, raven-black tresses, which hung to more than shoulder length, out of her luminous dark eyes. An observer, had one been present, might have put her age in her early twenties. Had such an observer been male, he would likely have been impressed by her fine, classically molded—though noticeably pale—features and her slender, well-formed figure.

As she stood silently resting, the wind, which cut through her cloak and thin white dress like a knife, carried the distant howling of a dog to her ears. Her dark, mobile brows raised quickly, and she listened alertly to the sound, gauging its distance. The animal had been disturbed by movement somewhere. It would be best to push on. Nervously, she moistened chapped lips with her tongue, tasting the saltiness of sheep's blood that had dried there...well, given the size of his flock, that beast's owner could well spare a single animal. Had her parents owned even a tenth part of such a flock, they would have counted themselves wealthy. Tears suddenly rose in her eyes as her mind saw vivid images of what her eyes would never see again. She saw visions of the snow-capped grandeur of a forested mountain in the Carpathians; the little thatched hut with the kitchen hut and beast shed behind it, the brook so quietly whispering beside it; and all the dear faces that looked on her with love. Impatient with herself, she wiped her tears on her sleeve with a swift motion, willing herself to concentrate on the present. She was here to stay in this flat, rainy foreign land, and right now what she needed was shelter and safety.

She moved forward again, taking care, wherever she could, to set her pigskin brogans down on rocks or frozen ruts that jutted above the snow, or to step into old tracks, so as to leave as little trail of her own as possible.

Fortunately, the blowing wind would erase much of what trail she did leave.

Her destination soon came into view. To her left down the crossroad, beyond the dark blocks of small houses—spill-over from the great city's growth—and the larger blocks of the smithy and the inn with its outbuildings, stretched the fenced, silent expanse of a graveyard. Its stone markers were mostly half buried by the white blanket that covered the ground. In the cemetery's middle, partly obscured by bare trees that grew all around it, stood a deserted chantry. Beneath it, in a musty, neglected crypt housing the forgotten dead, the protecting walls of a pine coffin, its bottom sprinkled with earth from a burial ground in distant Transylvania, waited for her.

Heart pounding dully inside her chest, Ana made her way down the road, glancing furtively at the buildings on her way, fearing the light of a candle in an unshuttered window. Movement to or from the chapel was always the worst part of these hunger-driven journeys, always beset by the fear of being seen. But she could not rent a lodging anywhere in which her comings and goings would not be questioned; she had no more money to rent with.

When she reached the burying ground's rusted gate, she took hold of the broken latch, silently eased the portal open a crack, then closed it behind her. Snow fell across her sleeve in the process. She brushed it away, then had to pause a moment to savor the shimmering, crystalline beauty of the snowdrifts where they gleamed in the moonlight. She had seen a few diamonds singly, in the jewelry cases at Castle Trina, but the snow was like hundreds of thousands of diamonds. What must it be like in the sunlight? She bit her lip, and lowered her eyes. She might imagine, but she would never again see what snow was like in daylight.

There was no cross atop the chapel now. Doubtless there had been one once, but it had long since fallen down. Ana knew there was one over the door, but she could not have crossed a threshold uninvited anyway. Before coming in view of the door, she angled away from the flagstone path and wound her way among the tombs. She turned frequently to brush over her tracks. A passerby would be able to tell that something had traveled here, but there would be no tell-tale footprints to say what—only a disturbance of the snow that could have been made by a stray dog, or a foraging fox or badger, wading through the white fluff.

An owl on the wing approached almost noiselessly from the darkness behind her, then challenged her with its plaintive, drawn-out hoot as it soared over her head on its way to a nest in the trees. *Rest well, friend owl,* Ana thought. *You and I are both hunters in the night, sleepers in the day. But you know no other life. Your rest is troubled by no memory of what you were, nor loathing of what you are. Sleep safely, feathered one.*

Approaching the building's near side, Ana arrived at a gap in the wall, a great jagged opening where the very stones had been hacked and levered out, from the foundation all the way to the roof. In the days of Henry VIII, when that monarch had led his people to break with the Church of Rome, a chantry was an inviting quarry for free building materials, offering folk a chance both to save money and to show their zeal against "Papist superstition." Several sections of the chapel's walls had gone in that fashion, as had half the roof and its supporting beams, the stained glass from the windows, even the altar and most of its woodwork. Ana wasted little time on thoughts about this dead history, fragments of which she had gleaned from drunken religious arguments overheard around the inn. *To my Orthodox upbringing, both Protestants and Catholics are exotics, and their disagreements of little meaning to me*, she thought somberly, when she could not bear even to look at the cross or hear the Name. She was just glad that their strife had left her a shelter with at least half a roof.

Stooping from habit, though the broken rain gutter hung several feet over her head, Ana entered the blackness of the chapel and took a few paces toward the stairs leading to the burial chamber below. Abruptly, she felt a mental warning bell as clear as the church bell back home in Nagy Timpa village. The chapel was too quiet. Ordinarily, even on a winter night, there were small animal noises here and there in the darkness, rodents scurrying back and forth, bats stirring in the rafters, sometimes a stray cat or dog foraging. But there were no such sounds now. Some presence had frightened the creatures, who by now were used to Ana, into silence.

Feeling her gut roil, Ana halted in her tracks, irresolute. If she turned and ran, where would she go? In less than an hour, the sun would be up. If there were someone in here with her, it might be only a vagrant seeking shelter. With a tongue suddenly gone dry, she licked at her lips, hoping she was removing any traces of blood. "Is—is anyone there?" she called in a trembling voice.

In the next instant, she was almost blinded by a sudden flash of light as someone removed a covering from a lighted lantern.

"Blimey, Will!" a coarse voice rasped. "You was right, you was!"

Her eyes not yet adjusted to the light, Ana was dimly aware of the shadowy forms of several men. Cold realization hit her in the face. Her survival was at stake, likely to be decided within seconds.

"Good morrow to ye all, good sirs," she spoke up, in the heavily accented English that was the best she could yet manage, even after months in this forsaken land. "I—I have traveled far this night, and thought to rest awhile in this place. I knew not that anyone was here, and crave your pardon for disturbing you. By your leave, I'll be on my way." As she spoke, she tried to sidle backwards toward the aperture she had entered through. Rough hands seized both her arms from behind before she had moved half a dozen paces.

"Be not so quick, wench!" snapped the one with the lantern. He moved closer and raised the light, shining it full on her face. She heard one or two of the men gasp. "Mayhap you can tell us why, if thou hast traveled so far this night, you have been seen entering and leaving here before—and why there be blood upon your mouth!"

"Aye, foul fiend," shouted another voice from behind the first speaker. "What helpless person did you slay to drink his blood?"

"No one," Ana cried truthfully. "No one at all, good masters! Upon my oath, I swear it!"

"What god would you swear by, demon?" a harsh voice demanded from the blackness. "Prithee, place your hand on this, and swear!" As the man moved into the arc of light, Ana saw by his vestment that he must be an Anglican priest. She saw, too, the crucifix, held on a chain around his neck, which he was now raising to the dim light and thrusting forward. The fear that had already gripped her was nothing compared to the sudden blind, unreasoning terror that now blotted out every other feeling.

She was half aware of a wild scream from someone—probably herself—but she had no time to think about it. Bringing her arms up and swinging them with all the considerable strength at her command, she sent the two burly men who had gripped her flying headlong into their companions. Curses and noises of falling bodies almost drowned the crash of the lantern shattering on the stone floor as the room returned to pitch darkness. Ana cast a quick glance behind her and saw two more figures silhouetted against the gap in the wall through which she had come. It was no matter; she must get to her coffin before sunrise, and now was her best chance, when the lightless confusion might hide her escape into the crypt...if only these men did not guess what that crypt contained.

Swinging wide, she broke around the melee of shouting men struggling to their feet and ran, with a sureness of movement that came from finding this way in the dark many times before, to the open head of the curving stair that led to the burial vault. A moment more, and she was lithely descending the uneven and broken steps two or three at a time. Once she gained the bottom, it was twenty medium paces to her right to reach the foot of her casket. She settled herself within, opening and closing the lid with practiced quietness. Her breath and heartbeat were loud in her ears in the confined space.

A cacaphony of confused shouting, some angry, some fearful, reached her ears. One harsh voice rapidly silenced all the others, apparently barking orders and encouragement. Rapid footfalls –many footfalls, moving in a menacing flood—began to surge toward the stairs.

Ana bit her lip, feeling the sweat trickle over her brow. There was no door on the crypt; door and hinges had been hacked off long ago to grace some new dwelling for the living. If they chose to search every coffin or sepulcher....   But they might not, for the English, unlike her people, knew little about the Undead and their needs. Feet were descending the stairs now. Should she lie still and hope for the best? Or should she leap up and make a fight of it? If she chose the latter course, it would surely mean killing in self-defense—and probably dying anyway. Not relishing either prospect, Ana closed her eyes for a moment as if to shut out reality, then opened them again. Probably best to lie where she was and keep quiet. There was a chance they would not risk a search that would disturb the dead—surely a chance, at least.

Now footfalls were clumping and shuffling over the floor of the crypt, moving closer and closer to where she lay. A voice rang out suddenly, jolting her nerves. "There be the coffin I found empty after the monster left at twilight! 'Tis not empty now, I'll warrant!"

Ana tensed for action, but before she could leap up, the coffin's lid was abruptly jerked open. The relighted candle from the lantern was instantly thrust over her face, almost blinding her, but she could see the outline of one other object inches from her eyes—the crucifix. Her whimper of terror was drowned by the roar of gloating anger and bloodlust that went up from the mob around her. She found the strength to cry out, striving to make her plea heard.

"Have mercy, good folk! What harm have I ever done any of you? I protest that I be innocent of wronging any soul—"

A mocking voice interrupted her. "Nay, 'tis but a poor harmless lamb thou art," the priest grated. "Vile limb of Satan, behold Him who is victor over such as you!" He thrust the crucifix down at her, grinding it painfully against her face. Mortal fear engulfed Ana's whole being with a cold, numbing force she had never imagined. She realized that she could not move—not a finger, not an eye muscle, not even her throat to so much as swallow, though in truth there was nothing in her bone-dry mouth to swallow.

One of the men staring at her perceived her sudden rigidity. "Look ye, and mark this," he cried gleefully.

"Aye, we 'ave 'er now, in sooth," answered the one with the candle. "What say you, Canon Fawcett—'ow do we finish her?"

The clergyman seemed to swell with self-importance. "Look you, Jack, fetch hither that sharp spar by the door and that half a brick beside it. In one of the books of lore I have, what she is be named 'vampyre', and in those pages is written the way to rid the earth of her—to drive a wooden stake square through her foul heart, that her flesh may rot away to nothing!"

"Here, your reverence," the one called Jack said, thrusting something into the man's hands. Ana caught a glimpse of an ugly-looking length of wood split from some forgotten sill or wall, one end tapering to a sharp, jagged point. Knowing what was about to happen, unable to make a single sound or movement to vent the sick horror that consumed her, unable even to close her eyes to shut out the sight, her only hope now was that the end would be quick. She forced herself not to think about whatever kind of beginning might wait on the other side of that end.

Now the wooden point was held against her left breast. As someone brought the brick down with both hands, searing pain sent a silent scream through her whole body. Once more, and again, the brick rose and fell. Her mind was swallowed in a black flood of ultimate, indescribable agony...and then the pain was suddenly gone, and she was toppling forward, abruptly aware of lurid light and a noise like a keg of gunpowder exploding. She fell onto a floor—not of stone, but of metal.

Chapter Two

Glad that the driving rain had paused for the moment, Joshua Davidson poked carefully through the charred debris inside the armored car's gutted storage chamber. Taffy-haired and six feet tall, with an athletic build, Joshua looked younger than his 24 years. Just now, he was looking intently for any sign of still-burning sparks or embers which might have escaped the dowsing from the hoses of Meriwether, Iowa's volunteer fire department. Most of the water-sodden ashes from the fire were behind him, closer to the vehicle's big back doors, which were now smashed beyond repair. The truck's contents at the very back had been spared the blaze—*and eerie contents they are, too*, he reflected, glancing down at the mummified body of a cat that lay at his feet beside its broken box. "It's all out, Cletus," he called to the chunky white-haired man who peered in from the rear.

"We're done, then," the fire chief replied, turning to call instructions to the handful of volunteers who had been at the station house when the alarm came, and the dozen or so others who, like Joshua, had come in their own vehicles after being summoned on their beepers. "You boys start gettin' that hose rolled up, pronto! I wanna get home."

At the edge of the fire's furthest inward reach, an overturned coffin lay across the floor, its badly charred bottom facing toward the double doors. Glancing down as he stepped around it, Joshua's keen grey eyes noticed something at the edge of his flashlight's beam. Frowning, he knelt beside the object. It appeared to be a wooden spar or stake, perhaps two feet long, broken off a larger piece of shaped wood, and tapering to a nasty-looking point. What caught the young man's attention was the black stain that covered about half the stake, from the point up.

"Mr. Masters, this looks like dried blood," he called to the security guard, who at the moment was standing beside Cletus. "Do you know how that would have happened?" He shined his flashlight on the item as he held it up to the older man's squinting gaze.

"Oh, that. Yeah, that'd be part of the cargo. This was a museum exhibit that had to do with witches and vampires, stuff like that. There was supposed to be a vampire's skeleton in the coffin there, and that'd be the stake they stuck through his ticker. It's on the inventory."

Looking down at the bloodstain, Joshua felt a wave of disgust at the thought that misguided, superstitious people could once have done such a thing to a fellow human, seeking to destroy something that didn't exist in the first place. He let the spar fall, and made his way back out of the compartment again, shaking his head.

By now, the fire fighters not responsible for the hose were clambering back into cars and trucks. Across the hardtop, the ambulance eased onto the wet road and headed back toward town. The siren was silent, for the driver of the armored vehicle was not seriously hurt, only cut slightly on the forehead.

Al Masters had followed Joshua's gaze. "Well, thank God at least we wasn't killed."

"Yeah," Joshua replied earnestly. "He blessed you guys real good there."

"Huh?" Al grunted, raising his bushy eyebrows and turning his head slightly. Joshua regarded him with mild surprise but had no time to reply before they were approached by the short, slight figure of Walter Andersen, Lewis County's solemn and officious deputy sheriff.

"Hey, Joshua, how are ya? Mr. Masters, Sheriff Saddler says he's going to need a statement from you. He's questioning the other driver right now, but you can wait in the squad car where it's dry. We'll give you a lift into town afterwards."

The security guard stared across the road toward a weaving, rain-soaked figure who was trying, without much success, to walk in a straight line under the eye of an equally wet, uniformed man. "You bet your sweet life I'll make a statement, and sign a complaint, too. That sucker's drunk as sure as I'm standin' here. This whole thing was his fault, the son of a—"

Joshua quickly interrupted him. "I'll walk over with you guys, Walter. I want to say hello to Tom." Walter pompously raised his hand to halt the movement of departing cars, and the trio crossed the hardtop, the guard stalking over to a parked squad car with a star on its door. A short distance away, "Jigger" Ficklin, chronic drunkard and barroom brawler, who worked as a bricklayer when he was sober enough to work, was attempting to present his account of the accident to Sheriff Tom Saddler.

"...Sho then I—I crawled out—outta my car to...get away from the fire, y'know, and then I shaw a bat fly—fly over me and fly away tha' way...or wash it thish way? It—it wash a very big bat, Sheriff."

"Did it happen to be pink, or was it purple with green stripes?" the sheriff asked drily.

Jigger, suspecting that his veracity was being impugned, regarded his questioner with injured truculence. "I—I don' know what color he wash," he replied thickly. "I can't—can't shee colorsh in the dark."

"Okay, Jigger, I reckon that'll do." Tom turned to his deputy. "Put him in the squad car, Walter, and take him in to the drunk tank. And see that he gets a blood test."

"Yes sir, Sheriff." Walter hauled the staggering man off by the arm.

Tom turned to his friend. A good-looking man of about 26, with dark hair and moustache, the sheriff was almost as tall as Joshua, and no less broad-shouldered and muscular. "Evenin', Josh. How're you tonight, besides soaked to the bone?"

"Oh, fair to middlin'. We haven't had this much excitement around here in a while, have we?"

Tom grinned ruefully. "I'd settle for boredom. I'm just glad nobody was killed, and it's a miracle nobody was. Jigger's windshield was shatterproof glass, an' he was belted in; otherwise he'd be dead right now. As it is, he's too soused to even know how close he came. Hey, is Molly workin' tonight?"

"Yes, she is," Joshua replied, with a twinkle in his eye. "If you have to stop by later for a medical report on that armored car driver, you'll probably see her." Molly Davidson, the older of Joshua's two sisters, worked a swing shift as an LPN at Lewis County Hospital in the small county seat town of Meriwether. She and Tom had been dating for about a year.

Tom's dark eyes showed an answering twinkle. "I expect I'll have to. You know how it is—a peace officer's work is never done."

"Well, I'm gonna get myself home and dry off. I'll see you at church if I don't happen to see you before."

"See ya around, Josh. Drive careful—this road's slick."

Acknowledging the parting caution with a nod, Joshua splashed down the road shoulder to where his battered blue Ford pickup was parked. The squad car pulled out and took off past him as he started the engine and turned his headlights on. As he eased the aging vehicle around onto the road, the rain began again, quickly swelling to nearly its former force. He glanced at his watch. It was 7:45. Being about fifteen miles from town as he was, he thought he ought to be home inside of a half-hour. With Molly working and his mother out of town, he'd have the house to himself. Right now, warming up with a hot shower and settling down on the sofa with a good book was an appealing prospect.

Gradually, the rain slackened to a steady, drizzling patter. Soon, Joshua saw that he was approaching the bend in the road, less than a mile from town, which diverted the hardtop from the old Rogers place. He could see the dark, ruined pile of the house straight in front of him. Its broken windows, half-fallen shutters and sagging porch were invisible in the rainy darkness but well-remembered from his boyhood days, when he and his schoolmates had dared each other to go up and knock on the door of the 'haunted' house. Having already slowed for the approaching turn, he suddenly touched the brake harder, easing the truck to a stop on the shoulder. In his brief glance at the deserted building, he had seen a light—faint, but certainly there nonetheless—moving across the inside of a window. And there—where the next window was—the light appeared again!

Curiosity kindled in the young man. What exactly was going on here? True, it was probably just a new generation of schoolboys scaring themselves—but it might be something more sinister that Tom should know about. And there was only one way to find out. He started to pick up his flashlight, then thought better of it. If there were drug dealers or something similar inside, there was no sense advertising his presence. Opening his door, he slid to the soggy ground, pausing for the moment by the truck bed to secure a stout wrench from the toolbelt there, just in case. Then, picking his way along the muddy, weed-grown footpath under dripping trees, he made his way toward the silently waiting ruin.

Chapter Three

Soaked to the skin by the rain, Ana plodded miserably along the shoulder of the road. Once she had put a good distance between herself and the flaming chaos from which she'd fled, she had taken human form again and returned to the road, several miles from where she had left it.

She hoped to meet some wagon driver or horseman who might let her ride with him to whatever town for which he was bound, where she could possibly trade her services in kitchen or stable for a night's lodging. The loss of her coffin, she thought, was not necessarily a fatal blow. So long as she was shielded from any ray of sunlight, and from any curious mortal, she could survive the next day and those that would follow. But questions nagged at her. As she now realized, her fleshly existence had been brutally interrupted in the crypt of the chantry. But for how long? It was no longer winter, so weeks or months, at least. And in what part of England was she now? What manner of vehicle had she been traveling in, and what had caused the fiery explosion which had knocked the stake from her chest and restored her to consciousness?

Answers did not suggest themselves. Impatiently, she wiped at the rainwater running down her face. Of course it rained at times in her homeland, but there, at least, it didn't rain practically all the time. Not like it did in this wretched....

She stopped to listen to a distant sound behind her, one she couldn't identify. It was different from thunder or wind. Its loudness rapidly increased. Turning, she suddenly became aware of a huge creature, much shorter than she, but very broad, its form obscured by rain and darkness, but its two huge yellow eyes shining with unnatural brilliance, racing toward her along the road. Not having time to be frightened, she slipped instantly as far back into the shadows as she could, covering herself as completely as possible with her pitch-black cloak, letting herself blend into the darkness. The strategy worked; the beast evidently did not see her, but rushed past and disappeared into the darkness ahead with unbelievable speed.

Now Ana's terror had time to assert itself. She remained for a minute or two, cowering and trembling in every part of her body, no more able to move than if she had been in a pillory. What was that thing? Was it a natural animal or a creature of some dark sorcery? Should she continue on in the same direction it had gone or turn back? But what if it had a mate who might be following behind it? And, she reflected, turning back would take her back toward whomever had held her prisoner and brought her here. Perhaps she should leave this road altogether...but if such beasts were bold enough to travel on the roads, was the open country likely to be any safer? Probably not.

The best thing to do, she thought, *might be to find some shelter and hole up inside it.* Forcing herself to move a few paces, she leaned against a tree to catch her breath. Her touch revealed that the trunk was unusually smooth, more like a shaped pole than a bark-covered tree trunk. She looked up and saw for the first time that it was indeed a manmade pole, one in a series of regularly-spaced poles behind and before her. They were connected by thick cables, reminding her of the rigging on the ship that had brought her from Varna to London. Her brows knit in puzzlement. She found herself unable even to form a speculation about the purpose of the bizarre arrangement.

She had not continued far before she made out the dark form of an unlighted building straight ahead of her. The road, she soon realized, made a bend which carried it around and past the structure rather than to it. Most likely the occupants were in bed, but perhaps if she knocked at their door they would grant her shelter in their barn. If she buried herself in the haymow, she might well be as safe there as anywhere else. Before she had gone many paces up the footpath, however, its overgrown condition made her suspect that the house was deserted. This was confirmed by a single glance at the structure itself in the sudden, brief illumination of a lightning flash. As the thunder died away, a slight smile crossed Ana's face. For her needs, this would be even better.

Scouting around quickly, she discovered that part of the house's north wall had buckled and partially collapsed. The yawning aperture thus created was amply large enough to admit her. Once inside, she removed her cloak and wrung it out, then wrung out the long, dripping locks of her hair. Soon, her eyes grew more used to the darkness, and she made out the outline of a fireplace in the far wall. Crossing over to it, she ran her long fingers over the cold stone of the mantel, and found the stub of a candle stuck to the surface by its own wax. It took only a few seconds to light it from her tinderbox.

She returned the small metal box to her pocket and then, holding the candle before her at a careful angle so that the hot wax dripped on the floor instead of her hand, began a more thorough inspection of the building's dark, empty rooms. Only the sound of her own footsteps broke the silence which reigned both upstairs and down. There was no furniture, only broken glass and wood scattered here and there, and drifts of dead leaves blown in through various holes. Festooning cobwebs hung everywhere, and gaps in the ceiling and roof upstairs showed the night sky. In a back room downstairs, Ana found what she had most hoped for: a door leading down, by worn stone steps, to a tomblike, windowless cellar. Its dirt floor would not be comfortable, but in her cataleptic state during the day she would not feel it. And with the door closed, no sunlight could penetrate the dank chamber.

It would be long hours before she would need this refuge, however. She retraced her steps up the stairs to the slightly less claustrophobic and depressing ground floor of the old ruin, wondering just how old it was, and how long it had lain empty. Had lovers' voices and children's laughter ever echoed on these walls, in some long-ago time before she was born?

Wandering into the first room she had entered, she stopped in her tracks, hearing the same indescribable growling sound outside that had preceded the appearance of the huge creature earlier. A quick glance through a broken window revealed another of the beasts—or perhaps the same one—in the road beyond. Could it smell her? At the same moment, Ana realized that the gleaming light from its huge eyes was so intense as to be reflected on the walls of the room in which she stood. Without wasting any time, her heart pounding like a mummer's drum on Harvest Day, she darted into a closet she had discovered earlier. Her candle was blown out as she slammed the door. The creature's growling fell silent, but she remained where she was, taking no chances.

After a few moments of deathly quiet, she was startled by the creaking of a floorboard under a foot. Too surprised at first to respond, she stood for a heartbeat or two in absolute immobility. Then the sound was repeated, and her usual self-possession asserted itself. Obviously the maker of the sound was human, not animal. She swung the closet door open, its hinges screaming in protest.

Through the gloom, she saw that the newcomer was a plainly-dressed man, fully as tall as she was, who seemed startled to see her, defensively clutching a stout tool he carried as if it were a weapon. "I mean you no harm," she reassured him quickly. "I did but hide in yonder closet for fear of a great beast outside with shining eyes, that growled fearfully. Mayhap you saw it too?"

He seemed to relax slightly at her tone, lowering his impromptu club slightly and peering at her closely. "Well," he said doubtfully, "I didn't see anything just now. A lot of folks around here have complained about wild dogs lately, though."

Ana shivered. "Verily, what I saw was too large to be any dog."

"Oh, some of those Great Danes and wolfhounds can get to be pretty big," was the reply. "Anyway, I thought I saw a light in the windows, and since I knew nobody lived here anymore, I decided to stop and see what's going on. My name's Joshua—Joshua Davidson. What's yours?"

"I am Ana Vasilifata," she answered, dropping in a curtsy. As she straightened, she thought she detected an unusual expression on his face, but in the darkness she couldn't be sure. "I was but traveling upon the highroad out there, and took shelter here from the rain. If it so please you, sir, do you likewise," she added. It had already occurred to her quick mind that this stranger might be a useful source of information about her whereabouts and new surroundings.

"I think the storm's slacking off some, now," Joshua answered. "But...I might wait a while and let it slack off some more. Uh, you aren't from this country originally, are you, ma'am?"

"Nay. My accent betrays that fact, I see." *Joshua's own accent*, Ana thought as she re-lit the candle, like his dialect, *is one I can't place*, despite having heard many of England's regional speech patterns in her months in the inns and alleys of London's poorer districts. Looking up, she saw the curiosity on his face in the newly kindled light. "Hast thou never seen a tinderbox before?" she asked banteringly.

"No," he replied, to her surprise. "It's neat, though. Do they use those much where you're from?"

"Aye, right much," Ana answered cautiously, giving him a searching look. Unease crept over her. First the strange, glowing-eyed creatures, now this grown man who seemed perfectly sane but had never seen a tinderbox...where in the world was she?

"Do you mind my asking where that is?"

"What?...Oh, nay, I mind not. I come from Transylvania. Know you of the place?" she added curiously as her questioner started visibly.

"I, uh, well, yes...that is, I know it was where Count Dracula was supposed to be from. But I always thought it was just make-believe, like he was."

Ana shivered again, recalling tales oldsters in Nagy Timpa had told her of her country's past. "'Tis not make-believe, Joshua Davidson, 'tis a very real land, with real people. Nor was Count Dracula, the Son of the Devil, make-believe. He was Voivode of Transylvania long ago, and they say no crueler man ever lived. He slew folk by the thousands. Many he impaled on stakes, so he was called Vlad the Impaler.. but that were too grim a tale to tell in the dark hours, in this lonely place. Come you, sir, sit down and rest you, and tell me of where you are from." She stuck the candle on a windowsill and,

27

undoing the thong of her cloak, spread the garment on the floor for them to sit on. "Dost thou live hereabouts?"

"I live in Meriwether—that's the county seat, less than a mile down the road," he answered, seating himself beside her. "I'm a carpenter."

Ana nodded. "I have traveled far, and I fear I be rather muddled in my directions. What large city is Meriwether most nigh to?"

"I suppose that'd be Davenport, if you go southeast. And Iowa City's not too far if you go southwest. Miss Vas...uh, do you mind if I call you Ana? I'm not sure I can pronounce your last name the way you did."

Something about his tone and manner kept Ana from taking offense at his rather forward request. "In sooth," she said after only a moment's pause, "you are not the only person in this land to find that difficult. You may call me Ana if it so please you, sir."

"If you keep calling me 'sir'," he responded with an engaging smile, "I'm going to start to feel like one of those old-time knights in armor. 'Joshua' will do. Ah—where did you learn to speak English, Ana?"

"In London, where I came after I left my homeland. No one taught me; I picked up what I could here and yon."

"That explains it, then," he exclaimed. "I never heard anyone speak English exactly like you do, and that must be because it's British English. My mom says when she hears English people on PBS, a lot of the time she can't understand half of what they say. I can understand you just fine, though. So, have you been in America long?"

When she did not answer, he stared at her more intently, in apparent concern. "Ana, are you all right?"

"Ah, I, yes...I, I am," she lied. Had a bottomless crevice suddenly appeared an inch from her toes on some mountain crag in her homeland, she could not have felt dizzier. America? The vast wilderness on the other side of the earth, where England had planted some small colonies? "I, I but felt a chill." She tried ineffectually to moisten lips suddenly gone dry, then shook with a real chill as a thought struck her. To bring her to an English-speaking colony in the New World would surely have taken many months. But did those colonies have any ruins this old? Just how long had it been since...? "What is the phrase folk use in your tongue–'someone walking over my grave?'" *Perhaps easier to do in my case than in most,* she thought bitterly. "Methinks these old walls have far too many holes to stop the cold. Know you, perchance, how old this house be, Joshua?"

"Well, I've heard tell it was built back in the days just before the Civil War, in 1859 or '60. That would make it...well, over a hundred and forty years old." As he went on, she realized she was staring at him, wide-eyed. More than 300 years! He was still speaking. "They say it belonged to a young couple named Rogers, who built it for a first home. But he was drafted into the Union army, and then got killed in one of the early battles. According to my grandma, his wife didn't want to live without him, so she hanged herself from one of the rafters there over the fireplace, and...." He broke off, glancing down at her trembling hands. "Boy, talking about grim tales in spooky settings! I'm sorry, Ana," he added gently. "I didn't mean to frighten you. It was all a long time ago. Anyway, the house has been empty ever since. I don't know who owns it now—maybe the county does, for back taxes."

"Th-then haply there be none who would object if I should bide here a little season?" she asked, thinking quickly, and surprised that she was able to speak with only a slight tremor to her voice. "Needs must I have some roof over my head whilst I earn some money...to continue my journey." A large city or its environs, where many folk came and went without knowing their neighbors, and where landlords asked few if any questions, was the safest place, she knew, for those of her ilk. But getting there intact would require some gold or silver, and so would renting lodging once there.

Joshua shook his head. "Nobody I know of would object. It sure isn't much of a roof, though...uh, what sort of work are you looking for?"

"If so be that I can," she answered, "I mean to take in sewing for folk." Her tinderbox held a needle as well as its other contents, and through the wet cloth of her dress she could feel the few spools of thread her other pocket held, rough against her legs. "My mother taught me to sew and embroider well, and no hands in Nagy Timpa village were more skilled than hers with a needle." Sudden moisture came to her eyes, and a lump rose in her throat.

"Your mom's passed away, then," Joshua said softly. "I'm sorry," he added simply when she nodded. "Mine's still living, but I lost my dad a few years ago. I think I know how you feel, Ana."

Something in his tone spoke to Ana's heart as well as to her ears. For a moment, she raised her dark eyes to look into his grey ones, then quickly lowered her own again, startled by the content and intensity of her thoughts. "So, how came you to be upon the roads on this wet night, Joshua? You have no carpenter's tools about you just now," she said hastily.

"Actually, I do have some in my truck," he replied, "but I wasn't coming home from work; I was coming home from a fire. I'm one of our town's volunteer firefighters, and we got called out for an accident down the road that way earlier tonight. A drunk driver rear-ended an armored car, and there was a gasoline explosion. The rain kept it from spreading, though."

Some of the words he used were meaningless to Ana, but she gathered easily enough that the accident to which he was referring was the one she had fled from. "Wast anyone hurt there?" she asked softly, raising her eyes again.

"Nobody seriously. The armored car driver got a gash across the forehead that'll take some stitches."

Ana nodded and then tried to make her tone sound casual. "Know you what this...armored car was carrying, and why?"

Joshua shrugged. "From what the guard said, it was some sort of museum exhibit from England that had to do with occult things. Kind of creepy stuff, at least what I saw of what was left was creepy. Most of it was burnt up, I guess." He fell silent, and Ana was suddenly aware that the patter of rain against the roof had ceased. She had become so accustomed to the sound, she realized, that she had not consciously noticed it until it was gone. "Our wet weather's rained itself out, I guess," Joshua said. From the undercurrent in his tone, Ana could tell that he rather wished it hadn't. "I suppose I'd better be getting along home."

"Aye—mayhap your wife will be anxious about you," she remarked impulsively, looking down to pluck imaginary lint from her cloak. *It is ridiculous*, she told herself sternly, *to feel any interest in his reply, one way or the other*.

"Since I'm not married," he said, rising, "that's not a problem, but I...should be leaving anyway. Oh, about your taking in sewing—neither my mom or my sister likes to sew, and mending sort of piles up around our house. More than likely I can bring you some tomorrow. How much do you charge?"

A warning bell sounded in Ana's mind. There was no way to know if the units of English money she knew were still in use here. "Ah, whatever 'tis worth to you, in sooth," she replied with a shrug. "I know little of the values of coins in this land, but you have an honest countenance, and I have no fear of being cheated by you. Come you at eventide tomorrow," she added, walking with him to the door, "and bring as much mending as your womenfolk will send. I shall be right glad of it."

"I'll plan on that. Ana, it was a real pleasure meeting you." He extended his hand, which she clasped a bit awkwardly, never having exchanged such a gesture with a man.

"Verily, the pleasure was mine," she said softly. "Good night to you, and a safe journey home." Shutting the door after him, she refrained from locking it—anyone could walk in through the fallen-in wall, anyway—and stood a moment listening to his receding footsteps. Then, increasingly aware of the night chill, she walked back to where her cloak lay and picked it up again, her touch lingering on the warm spot where the young man had sat.

Werner Lind

Chapter Four

Freshly shaved and clad in his work clothes, Joshua bounded down the stairs. Morning sunlight streamed into the hallway, and the smell of frying bacon greeted his nostrils. His sister was up and busying herself with breakfast. Striding rapidly through the front room, he entered the simply-furnished, high-ceilinged kitchen. "Good morning, Sis!" he said cheerfully.

Molly Davidson raised her good-natured, light green eyes long enough to nod to her brother. A year younger than Joshua, she was short and stout, with auburn hair worn in two braids. Where his looks favored their mother's side of the family, hers favored their father's. Nonetheless, a close observer could see a family resemblance in the general shape of their features—and a kinship of spirit in the optimistic good humor of their usual expressions. "Good morning, yourself," she answered. "You're just in time. Breakfast's ready."

She slipped into her place across from him, and both bowed their heads as he recited a short grace. Joshua attacked his eggs and bacon with relish. "So, did that armored car driver get stitched up all right last night?"

"Oh, yeah. It wasn't anything too serious—they handled it on an outpatient basis. Dusty Rhodes and his photographer made a real nuisance of themselves, though, taking pictures of the driver and wanting to interview anybody who worked on the guy. It seems old Mr. Rhodes is going to play this accident up big in the paper when it comes out Thursday. In fact, Dusty said the old guy told him he was going to call it in to the wire service."

Joshua raised his brows. "Why? Except for the museum people that owned the stuff that burned, who outside this county would care about it?"

"Apparently the exhibit had attracted a lot of attention in some of the big cities back East where they showed it already, and there had been quite a bit of advance publicity for it on the West Coast. Dusty said his dad believes that if they play up the occult angle— because of all the weird stuff the car was carrying, you know—it would be a big human interest story. He said lots of readers would eat up a story that hinted at disappearing skeletons, car crashes maybe caused by witches' curses, stuff like that."

Joshua just snorted. "The crash wasn't caused by a curse," he said shortly. "It was caused by a driver so drunk he was seeing things. If that's a big human interest story, it doesn't take much to interest some people."

The tea kettle whistled, and Molly rose to pour water for her decaffeinated coffee. "Well, obviously it doesn't, when you consider how fast those tabloids sell out down at the I.G.A. Besides, they're also going to play up the idea that something dangerous might have escaped in the accident. They're doing that tongue-in-cheek, of course, but Dusty said it would still sell papers. Not to change the subject, but are you going down to Cranesville today to start tearing down the old hatchery?"

Joshua nodded as he swallowed a large mouthful. "Yeah, I want to get started on it. I'm working under a deadline if I want to get my bonus. Why?"

"Because I made your lunch just in case. It's in the fridge. Is the deadline because they can't start putting up the new convenience store 'til the hatchery's down?"

"No, it's going up closer to the side street, and I expect Wade will have his crew there today to start on the foundation. But they can't gravel the rest of the lot for a parking lot 'til the hatchery's gone. Hey, Molly, how would you like to get rid of the mending in the bag upstairs?"

"I would, but when Mom gets home tonight, I don't think she'd take kindly to finding it in the trash," Molly replied dryly. "Or did you want to volunteer to sew it?"

"No, I've got an idea that's more pleasant, and that lets us help someone who needs to earn money. On my way home from the fire last night, I saw a light at the old Rogers place, and stopped to check it out. I met this foreign girl about my age; she's traveling cross-country—hitchhiking, I guess, since I didn't see a car around—and she wants to take in sewing to raise some traveling money. She said we could just pay her whatever we thought was fair."

Molly listened to this recital with a skeptical frown. "I don't know. How do you know...well, I guess she wouldn't want to steal torn clothes. You say she's foreign? What country is she from?"

"Uh, she said she's from Transylvania," Joshua answered, clearing his throat. Molly stared, then burst into a laugh.

"Okay, you got me," she admitted cheerfully. "You kept such a straight face I didn't figure that this was one of your jokes."

Shaking his head, Joshua set down his glass. "No, Molly, it's not a joke. I know it sounds like one, because of the accident and all the silly talk, but that's just a coincidence. I really did meet this woman. You can meet her tonight yourself if you want; we could go after I get back from the bus station with Mom. And she's really a nice person. And Transylvania's a real place, too; I looked it up in the atlas after I got home last night. Actually, it's not a country—it's part of Romania—but it's on the map."

After pursing her lips thoughtfully, Molly shrugged. "Okay, if you say so. I don't mind hiring her to do some sewing for us if Mom doesn't object." She smiled impishly, looking down at her plate. "Does your sudden interest in our mending have anything to do with wanting to see this pretty girl again?"

"Of course not!"

Molly nodded solemnly. "I see—she's not pretty, then?"

"I should say she is," Joshua retorted indignantly. "She's pretty enough to be a model in a magazine, with the sweetest eyes...." He broke off, catching sight of his sister's grin. Going to the refrigerator, he took out his lunch. "I've got to get going. Anyway, I'd say she's every bit as good-looking for a woman as, oh, who would be a good example? As, say, Tom Saddler is for a man," he added, succeeding in keeping a straight face. The next instant, with practiced quickness, he ducked the wadded-up paper towel playfully thrown at him by his sister, and the sound of their laughter floated through the house.

* * * *

Noon found Joshua busily engaged in prying nails from the last row of shingles on the Main Street side of the old Fry's Hatchery in Cranesville, a hamlet about nine miles southeast of Meriwether. Turning his head to the east, he could see the mile-wide expanse of the Mississippi only a block away, its slowly flowing waters still high at this time of year, and appearing, in this light, as a silvery blue. On another day, Joshua knew, or even at another time on the same day, they might appear pure blue, unmixed silver, golden brown, or muddy brown. His reflections on the beauty of creation were interrupted by the harsh bellow of Wade Bruggenhorst, whose curses rose abruptly over the rumble of the cement mixer to Joshua's right. There the Bruggenhorst construction crew was preparing the foundation for the convenience store which was to face the Locust Street side of the Fry corner property. Wade was, Joshua guessed, swearing at his son Itchy.

"Watch where you push the wheelbarrow, ya moron!" the older man finished, when he had apparently run out of expletives. "Is that too much to ask, even for you? Is it?"

"Where the—where did ya want me to push it?" responded the sullen, grating voice of Joshua's former grade school classmate. Though a year older than Joshua, Itchy had flunked second grade, and had been a year behind through the rest of his schooling, until he dropped out.

"I don't want it pushed across my foot! Judas Priest, are ya tryin' to kill me? Tim, turn that thing off! It's time to knock off for lunch anyway. Josh! Hey, Josh!" He advanced to the foot of Joshua's extension ladder to holler up at him. "You ain't et yet, have ya?"

"No. I haven't," Joshua answered, methodically sorting straight and bent roofing nails into separate pockets of his leather apron.

"Well, come on down and eat with us, then, if ya want to."

"I'll be right down. Stand clear—shingles coming down." Joshua dropped a last batch of shingles to the ground to join the piles already there waiting to be gathered and hauled to the landfill. Descending the ladder, he fetched his lunch pail from the pickup and crossed the almost trodden-to-death grass to join Wade and the other three men seated on cinder blocks beside the newly-forming foundation. He seated himself quickly, bowing his head for a short, silent grace. As he opened his lunch, Wade's journeyman, Tim O'Connor, spoke up.

"That was some excitement we had for a while last night, eh, Josh?" Tim also belonged to the volunteer fire unit. "Up until then, we ain't had a fire yet this year."

Joshua nodded, pausing before biting into his ham and cheese sandwich. "I'm just glad nobody was hurt seriously, and that it was too wet for the fire to spread to the grass before we got there. That could've been a real mess in dry weather."

"What fire?" grunted Wade's unskilled helper, Lennie "Bull" Reevis, his dull-witted eyes suddenly wide with curiosity. "I ain't heard about no fire."

"Don't you listen to the morning news on the Davenport radio station?" Tim said.

"Naw! I don't listen to nuthin' but heavy metal, man!" Bull snapped, as if insulted to be suspected of an interest in current events.

Wade snorted, working the perpetually brown-stained corners of his mouth. "Well, I heard it, and I thought it was a bunch of cussed foolishness. You'd think that announcer was some kind of retard, talkin' about witches' curses and vampire skeletons. And if Jigger don't make bail by the time I'm ready to have the brick laid on this job, I'm through with him. If he had a brain in his head, he'd a' learnt by now, drinkin' and drivin' don't mix. I told him so often enough, and this ain't the first time he's pulled a stunt like this."

"Will somebody tell me about the fire?" Bull demanded.

"Jigger rear-ended an armored car carryin' a whole bunch of far-out stuff that had to do with witches and spooks and such in the old days," Tim said, "and they were sayin' on the radio that some people might wonder if it didn't crash because of some kind of curse on it, or if some kind of spooks didn't escape. I mean, the announcer didn't say he thought that, mind you, just that there was folks that would. I saw some of the stuff myself before it burnt—I was one of the first ones in there with the hose—and it was enough to make ya wonder, I tell ya. I seen this skull with a spike hammered in the top of it, and flames all around it, and this thing like an open mummy case with razor blades stickin' up out of it. I didn't see the vampire skeleton, though. That evidently burnt up. And they said on the radio that that was kinda strange, 'cause bone doesn't usually burn. They found the coffin it was in, and the stake that was supposed to have been in the old vampire's pump." Joshua had seen both of these, but kept silent, not willing to contribute fuel to the discussion.

Itchy broke in on Tim's monologue. "What if that thing was a real vampire, and he got loose somehow?" he said, half-chewed food showing as he spoke. He reached up to rub his dark, greasy hair with dirty fingers. Joshua wondered fleetingly if Itchy's habit of rubbing or scratching his head had given him his nickname. In any case, "Itchy" was the only appellation by which he was ever addressed.

"There ain't no vampires," Wade snapped. "Everybody on God's green earth that has half a brain knows that, except you!"

"How do you know there ain't?" Itchy retorted.

"'Cause the scientists don't believe in 'em, that's how. Itchy, wake up and smell the coffee, for cryin' out loud. Them scientists nowadays know pert near everything. If they know enough to send rocket ships to the moon, they'd know enough to find vampires, if there was any such things to find!"

"Well, I know what I saw with my own eyes," Itchy said with dogged assertiveness, "and I seen this old vampire guy that went around bitin' broads in the throat. He was in a movie a couple years ago at the drive-in; I was there with Alice Reed—"

Bull snickered. "You went to the drive-in with Easy Alice," he said, as he picked his nose and then wiped his finger on his shirt, "and you watched the movie?"

"I had to let her up for air once in a while, didn't I?" Itchy snapped at the burly youth. "Anyway, they tracked him down at the end and pounded this big old stake through his heart with a mallet, and did he ever scream. I'm tellin' ya, he screamed so ya could've heard it for miles. And bleed—man, he bled buckets. They showed the blood squirt up outta his chest every time the hammer come down, and it ran out his mouth and nose and eyes, even out his ears." He paused to enjoy the memory, his face taking on a glow of almost sexual pleasure.

"Man, that'd be a kick to make somethin' scream and bleed like that. Ya could get a better buzz offa that than offa booze, any day of the week."

Joshua had gulped the last of his lemonade. "Well, it's back to the salt mines for me," he said shortly, returning his thermos to his lunch pail. "Don't you guys work too hard, now."

Wade snorted. "Not much danger of that with this bunch."

As he moved toward his ladder, Joshua shook his head. *Not all monsters in this world,* he mused, *are found in movies.*

Chapter Five

Coming suddenly awake from a dreamless state of suspended consciousness, Ana opened her eyes amid total darkness and lay still for a moment recollecting where—and when—she was. Then she rose stiffly to her feet, yawned, and stretched. As she had feared, her clothes and brogan shoes were still slightly damp, but at least they were no longer sodden with moisture. She picked up and donned the cloak on which she had slept, brushing the dust of the dirt floor from her garments as well as she could in the dark.

Her belly growled insistently, and she bit her lip lightly. Before dawn, she should feed. But that could wait several hours, until full darkness had been upon the land for some time and most humans were asleep. She made her way unerringly across the dark basement to the stairs, mounted them quickly, unbolted the cellar door, and stepped into the only slightly less dark ground-floor hallway of the old house, which, she reflected, had not even been built when she.... Unconsciously, she touched the spot on her breast where the stake had gone in, shuddering at the horrible memory.

And in what sort of world did she find herself now? Rubbing her chin thoughtfully, she sat down on the lowest step of the stairway that led to the second floor. Last night, moments after Joshua had left, it had been a shock to discover, when she had looked out the window in terror at the sound of one of the bright-eyed creatures returning, that the 'creatures' were actually some sort of vehicle, and that Joshua rode in one. Her first thought had been that these self-propelling vehicles must be instruments of black magic, powered by some demonic sorcery. But she had looked deeply into Joshua's eyes as he sat beside her on her cloak, and instinctively she knew that the man behind those eyes was not in league with the devil. The conclusion she had eventually reached, she was sure, had to be right. Some scholars, so the priest at Nagy Timpa had once said in her hearing, believed there was such a thing as 'natural magic', neutral forces of mystery, such as the power in a lodestone or the attraction that drew a divining rod to water. These were not generated by the devil, but simply built into the order of creation, and could be used without sin by those who knew how to do so. Evidently, the time to which she had come was one in which such natural magic was more widely understood and used than it had been in the time she left. At first seemingly incredible, upon reflection this idea did not appear so far-fetched. And, after all, she could hardly doubt the testimony of her own eyes. Her brows knit in a frown. Such a world would be a dangerous one for her. No doubt people living here took for granted much knowledge she did not possess, and her lack of it might be hard to explain convincingly.

She rose and paced across the bare floor. The less she had to do with people, the better. That had been true ever since she had become what she was, but it was now truer than ever. Yet she would need some human contact to earn the money she needed for travel and lodging. This thought made her recall Joshua's promise to return with some sewing for her. Probably it would not be long before he came.

No sooner had she formed this thought than she heard the distant noise of a self-propelled vehicle approaching on the road, from the direction in which Joshua had gone the night before. That did not necessarily mean that this vehicle was his. But as she watched the speedily-moving conveyance from the vantage point of a broken window, she saw it slow as it rounded the bend in the road, and heard it stop in front of the house. She moved to the front door and pressed herself against it, listening. The feeling of butterflies in her stomach she was now experiencing was, she told herself, completely natural given the stress of her strange and dangerous situation.

More than one pair of feet, she soon realized, were coming up the path. As they reached the porch steps, she opened the door. In the lingering twilight, she saw that one of the visitors was Joshua. The other two were women, but the younger of these was dressed like a man, in shirt and pants. Ana managed to hide her surprise and mumble a greeting, but forgot to curtsy until it was too late. She kicked herself mentally for the lapse.

"Hello, Ana," Joshua said, with a ready smile. "It's good to see you again. I brought you the mending I told you about." He handed her a large brown paper bag he was carrying, full to the top with socks and other garments or cloth articles. "We'll pay you fifty dollars to do it for us, if that's all right with you?" When she nodded, he went on. "And my mom and my sister wanted to meet you, so I brought them along."

Ana's first impression of the masculine-garbed younger woman who now stepped forward was of her differences from Joshua in size and coloring, but a closer glance revealed a more subtle resemblance as well. When the newcomer smiled, the likeness was heightened. "Hi, Ana," she said. "I'm Molly, and I'm glad to meet you. This is my mom, Mrs. Mary Davidson."

"Just plain Mary will do well enough," the older woman interjected gently. Turning her eyes from Joshua's sister's odd clothing, Ana noticed for the first time that though his mother was at least clad in a dress, the skirt, like a prostitute's, reached only to her knees. However, the woman's bearing and expression held no hint of lewdness. Colored much like Joshua, with grey eyes and hair turning from straw-colored to grey, she radiated an air of kindhearted benignity that reminded Ana of her own grandmother. "Hello, Ana," she went on, extending a circular object wrapped in metal foil that glinted in the twilight. "My daughter here made too much food for supper tonight, so I was wondering if you could take this off our hands. I do so hate to see food go to waste."

As Ana was well aware, there was no way her stomach would accept whatever food was on the plate, and she opened her mouth to make some excuse for refusing it. But as she looked into her benefactress' face, she changed her tack. "Thank you much, good mistress. I shall be well-pleased to eat it and grateful to you." *After all*, she thought, as she reached out and took the plate, *these people won't know whether I eat the food or not*, and accepting it would arouse less suspicion than a refusal. "I would invite ye in," she added, "but, indeed, I have no chairs to offer, and the floor here be dirty beyond measure."

"We quite understand, dear," Mrs. Davidson answered. "I only wish you had better accommodations...." She trailed off, studying Ana's face for a moment in the failing light, then spoke again with a sudden air of decision. "With several of my children moved away from home, we have more than one empty room at our house. Perhaps we could work out some arrangement, so you could have a better roof over your head than you have here."

Though touched, Ana immediately shook her head. "You—you are most kind, in sooth," she stammered, "But I cannot accept so generous an offer. Verily, I am too much in debt to ye all already. But I thank you heartily."

"Well, if you say so. But let me know if you change your mind, and we'll see what we can do," was the reply. "Now, I want to pay you in advance for the mending." Reaching into her pocket, she took out a sort of wallet, from which she extracted some rectangular pieces of paper and handed them to Ana. "Will it be all right if I send my son to pick it up in a few days?"

Ana met Joshua's eyes briefly, then looked away, somehow embarrassed. She had no good reason to be, she told herself sternly. "Of course. I shall start on it straightway. Know ye of any place nearabouts where I might buy a candle or two? I, uh, may do some of the sewing by night."

"A candle or two?" the woman repeated blankly, then added, "Oh, of course. This old place isn't wired for electricity, is it?"

Now it was Ana's turn to stare somewhat blankly. Just then, Joshua spoke up. "Here—I have something that'll work a lot better than candles!" Turning, he ran to his vehicle, opened the door, and hurried back with an object. Ana set her sack and plate down inside the door to accept the offered item. "I'll be glad to loan you this electric lantern while you're here—I don't use it very often. It's battery operated, and fully charged. You can just stand it up like this, and press this switch." As he demonstrated, the porch was suddenly bathed in light as bright as noonday. To hide her amazement, Ana dropped her eyes, raising them a moment later when she felt her expression was under control.

"Again, I thank you, Joshua. This lantern of yours will be most welcome...." Abruptly, she froze for an instant. Her glance had happened to fall on Mrs. Davidson's dress front, and there, illuminated in the unnatural light, was an object Ana had been unable to discern before: the tiny but unmistakable shape of a gold cross, dangling from a thin chain. The same icy, blinding terror she had known in the ruins of the chantry possessed her again.

Joshua's voice sounded dimly in her ears, as if from far away. "Ana! Are you all right? Do you feel sick?"

With her wits benumbed by fear, and her mouth suddenly feeling as if it were filled with wool, Ana struggled to answer. "I...nay. I mean, yes. I feel...a faintness. It cometh upon me at times," she added, gripping the doorknob until her knuckles were white, and raising her other trembling hand to forestall Joshua as he started toward her. "I—I must but go apart and rest for a little season, then shall I be well again. Pray you, excuse me!" Hastily she closed and bolted the door, turned, nearly tripping over the dropped lantern, and ran, stumbling as she went. She did not stop until she slumped to her knees, her chest heaving like a blacksmith's bellows and her whole frame shaking convulsively, against the farthest wall of the cellar.

* * * *

Hours later, her paralyzing terror long past, though it left behind considerable worry over what suspicions it might have aroused in her callers, Ana found herself on the stone footpaths of the town Joshua had called Meriwether. Worry had to take second place in her attention now; it was overshadowed by her growing need to appease the thirst in her belly. She had set her face resolutely toward the town, where, she reasoned, stray cats, small starveling dogs, and rats should provide abundant prey. Livestock, of course, would be much more abundant out in the country, but such beasts were apt to be protected by human shepherds, or at least by fierce and noisy dogs of the large and well-fed sort. Besides, Ana's conscience shrank from killing any farm beast on which a poor family might really depend. Much of the distance from the old house had been covered in flight, but she had resumed human form on the edge of the town, along the streets of which she had now been walking for some time.

What she was now experiencing, she reflected with spine-tingling awe, was a reality she could never have dreamed of seeing in her wildest flights of fancy: a world three centuries and more removed from her own, much of it as alien to anything she had ever known as the sleeping streets of some town in Araby or Cathay—yes, even some town on the moon—would have been. By the position of the moon, she guessed it was an hour or so past midnight, but she could see the scene around her as if it were daylight. Strange lamps, not unlike the gleaming lights on the self-propelled vehicles, were mounted on tall poles at intervals all along the ways and byways. Their weird light paled that of the moon and shed an unnatural, day-bright illumination over everything. Indeed, Ana thought, this illumination was much too brilliant to suit her primary purpose, although so far she had found no one stirring on street or path, and the houses she had passed on her way into the heart of the town had all been dark. These houses had been for the most part rather large, some of them almost palatial, built of wood or brick, most with large porches, many of them decorated with flowers in pots or beds, and nearly all set on green lawns. Space evidently was not scarce here.

Now, having crossed a wide side street with strangely smooth stone pavement, Ana found that houses were replaced by closely set structures that were clearly stores and shops, most with large glass windows displaying their owner's wares. She could recognize the nature of some of these establishments from the sort of goods they displayed—cakes and sweetmeats in one; clothing in another, ingeniously displayed on life-sized figures that were clearly the work of a very skilled carver; and shoes in another. But she could not read the English letters on any of the signs, any more than she could have read words even in her native Romanian. She missed the usual symbols and pictures that would announce a shopkeeper's business to unlettered folk like herself, though she did recognize a barber's pole across the street.

The night chill made her shiver slightly, and she drew her cloak more tightly around her. Some ways beyond the barber shop gaped the entrance of an alley. Unlit as they were, the alleys were a good deal darker than the streets, and should offer a much better hunting ground. Moving as soundlessly and alertly as a lynx in her native forests, Ana crossed the street and entered the shadowed gap between the buildings. After taking only a few noiseless steps, she heard low whispers some yards ahead of her, and made out two figures in the weak moonlight. Instantly, she flattened against the brick wall nearest her. Then, drawn by curiosity, she began to inch forward silently, keeping herself in the darkness.

Within moments, she could distinguish the words and voices of the whispered dialogue. A male voice sounded grating and unpleasant. "I'm tellin' ya, baby, I ain't sellin' ya any pot on credit, and that's final! I'm in the business to make money—"

He was interrupted by an angry female voice. "Ya gave me plenty of freebies when ya got me started on the stuff, though, didn't ya?"

"That was good business, then, dollface," the first speaker replied imperturbably. "It ain't good business now. Hey, I go to all the work of findin' where this stuff grows an' pickin' it an' all—I gotta get somethin' for my time, ya know? But it don't hafta be money—not if you was to give me somethin' better. Then we might could deal."

For a moment, the female voice hesitated. "I don't know what you're talkin' about, Itchy—"

"Yeah, ya do," came the reply, and Ana could feel the lechery in the rough voice, almost like a slimy physical touch. "You be nice to me, and I just might be nice to you—if you're good enough."

By the tone of the answering voice, the speaker was near tears. "No, Itchy, please! I don't wanna—I told my boyfriend he'd be the only one. Please, just give me one little bag. I'll get ya the money Friday when my mom gets paid, I swear—"

Itchy's cold tones interrupted her. "Take your clothes off, or I'll take 'em for ya! And don't even think about hollerin', or I'll see that your mom—an' the sheriff—find out all about our little business deals!"

"Enough!" Ana's voice slashed across the scene like a whip crack. While she had not understood all of what she had heard, she had understood enough of it. Anger swept through her mind like the torrents of melting snow in the Carpathians, pouring down to swell the peaceful creeks into deadly, raging floods. She stepped from the shadows into the dim light that fell from the lamp near the alley's entrance, closing the gap between herself and the human pair with swift, long-legged strides. "There shall be no rape here tonight," she declared commandingly.

At the sight of Ana, the girl—for judging by her voice, she was fairly young—let out a hastily suppressed shriek and bolted in the opposite direction, not looking back until darkness had swallowed her retreating figure. But the coarse-voiced male stood his ground, and even took a step toward Ana. That motion brought his face into what light there was. It was not an appealing sight. Dull-witted, malicious eyes glinted above a flat, hairy nose and snarling mouth, in a sallow, pitted face. He growled an obscenity that Ana had heard once or twice in the back streets of London, which made her eyes and lips narrow in a cold fury more dangerous than the heat of her already kindled indignation.

"You will do well to mind your tongue, sirrah," she said, keeping her voice quiet and level with an effort, "Lest haply you come to grief."

"No, you got that wrong, baby-doll," he grated in reply, keeping his tone low as well. He no more wanted to attract the attention of night watchmen or passers-by than she did, Ana realized with a quickening surge of boldness. "You just bought yourself more grief than you ever figured on, ya know? See, you heard some stuff that wasn't your business, and I ain't gonna let ya just walk away from it. An' I was all stirred up for some fun that you just yanked out from under my nose. That wasn't very friendly, was it? Whaddaya think I'm gonna do about that, huh? Maybe you got a suggestion, huh?" The last question was delivered with a sneering note of menace that left no doubt as to his intentions. As he spoke, he fumbled in one pocket. Ana heard a slight, metallic clicking noise, then saw a long, wicked-looking blade snap erect in his hand. *A very handily carried weapon*, she thought scornfully—*doubtless prized most by footpads and cutpurses.*

"Foul, misbegotten mound of walking donkey dung!" she spat. "Think you that I fear you—a bullying dolt without courage or honor, pretending to himself to be a man?"

Even in the poor light, Ana could see his face redden. "I'm gonna get a kick outta this," he growled, lunging forward and grabbing for her wrist with his free hand. With a voiceless grunt, he abruptly bent double.

She had met his rush with a lightning-swift kick, which sent her foot squarely into his straddle. Her next kick, delivered while he was bent over, caught him full in the face with force enough to land him on his back. In an instant, Ana had gripped his left wrist with a viselike lock. Pulling him partly up, she slammed his right hand into the side of the nearest building, forcing him to drop the knife; then, turning him to face away from her, she bent his right arm in a hammer lock and transferred the forceful grip of her other hand to the back of his neck. "Cease your struggling," she ordered, "or I will break it like a twig!"

Instantly, he obeyed, going still in her grip. "Uh, ma'am," he whispered with suddenly-adopted meekness, "What're ya gonna do?" Bent over him, holding him to his knees, with her mouth not far from the back of his unwashed neck, Ana had to fight for her usual self-control, and did not answer. "Uh, er, ma'am? Ya do know I was just sorta kiddin' around with ya just now, don't ya? An' I was just kiddin' around before with Kay, too—her an' me's friends, we kid each other a lot, ya know? 'Bout that pot in the bag,"—he gestured as best he could with his head, and Ana glanced down at a bag of some transparent material whose contents showed, even in the poor light, as green in color—"ya ain't gonna turn me in to the sheriff for that, are ya? Tell ya what—how about I just give it to ya for free?"

"Be still," Ana said curtly. What manner of herb was it he had in that bag? Whatever it was, it commanded some form of sorcery which gave him a kind of power over the girl he had threatened. Doubtless it was some type of black magic. Were it of the innocent natural sort, he would not fear the sheriff. Back in England, witchcraft had been a hanging offense, and probably was so here, too. True, she could not report him, but.... She dragged him over the ground to where the bag lay. "Eat it," she ordered. "You'll not give it to anyone else."

"B-b-but, ma'am," he stammered, "ya don't eat pot—"

"Nay, and I shall not. But you will. Now." She bore down a bit harder on his neck for emphasis.

Whimpering a little, and gagging and choking as he obeyed, he shoved the green leaves into his mouth, chewed awkwardly, and gulped them down with a shudder. Having released his right hand so he could feed himself, Ana used her free hand to seize his greasy hair and turn his head around, bringing their faces a few inches apart. The sight of blood running from his bruised nose made her mouth water. She swallowed hard, letting her eyes bore into his. She saw no genuine penitence there, only fear and hate.

"You are called Itchy," she stated quietly, remembering how the girl had addressed him. He nodded. "Itchy, heed well my words," she said, underlining the sentence with a slight increase of pressure on his neck. "I could slay you as easily as I could break a rotten thread, did I wish to. I take no delight in killing, so I will let you live—now. But I make no promise as to what I shall do if you menace me again, nor if I needs must protect someone else from you. Dost thou understand me?"

"Yeah...I, I mean yes, ma'am—ya talk funny, but I can still understand ya...I mean, no offense about how ya talk—"

"Have you a home hereabouts?" she interrupted. When he nodded, she added, "Then get you there, and bide 'til dawn. And find yourself some other trade than black sorcery!" With a shove from which she held back much of her full strength, but which still sent him sprawling several yards deeper into the alley, she released him. He picked himself up without a word and ran. In moments, she could neither see his back nor hear his footsteps.

Trembling as her nerves at last reacted to the stress of the situation, she wiped the hands that had touched him on the skirt of her dress. Her glance fell on the knife he had drawn. Bending and seizing it, she broke it in two at the place where the blade extended from the handle, then hurled the pieces into an open bin which her nose told her held garbage. She took two or three deep breaths, letting her anger ebb from her. After a few moments she turned, moving as soundlessly as her shadow, and retraced her steps toward the street.

Werner Lind

Chapter Six

The telephone startled Joshua as he raised his cup at the breakfast table. "I'll get it," Molly said, rising quickly to cross the room to the wall phone. "Oh, hi, Tom!" she said, suddenly beaming.

Mary Davidson exchanged a knowing smile with her son. "They do seem to get along well, don't they?" she observed, lowering her voice. He nodded, then frowned as this train of thought somehow brought Ana to mind. Glancing across the table at him, his mother raised her brows.

"I was just thinking about Ana again," he said, answering the unspoken question. "That sick spell she had yesterday has me worried. It came on her so suddenly, and she was really in a lot of distress. It makes me wonder if she needs some kind of medical attention."

Mrs. Davidson wiped her mouth with a paper napkin. "Well, I've given that sick spell a lot of thought, too, and I believe I know what caused it. I think the poor girl's simply suffering from hunger. She obviously doesn't have much money, and she probably hasn't been able to afford to eat properly—or at all, perhaps. If that's the problem, that plate of food we took to her should help, and so should the fifty dollars. Which makes me glad I decided to pay her in advance; I hadn't planned to, at first."

"Joshua," Molly interjected, "Tom wants to know if you want to go fishing with him at Clay Creek on Saturday. His car, his place, at dawn."

"Tell him he's on. We'll plan on catching our supper." Joshua turned back to his mother. "Maybe that is what caused it," he said doubtfully. "It would explain why she's so pale. Do you think Doc O'Riordan should have a look at her? I mean, if she had to go without food for a long time, could she have any kind of damage from malnutrition that might need medical care?"

"She was well enough to walk some distance the night before last, evidently," his mother said. "I doubt if anything is seriously wrong with her. She probably just needs some food and some rest. What do you think, dear?" she asked, as Molly rejoined them.

Molly sighed, her face almost beatific. "I think he's the nicest guy I've ever dated, not to mention the best looking. We're going to the drive-in Saturday night. There's a double feature."

Her mother shook her head in good-natured exasperation. "I mean, what do you think about Ana? You're a nurse. Could her sick spell last night have been just faintness from hunger? And if it was, should we be worried about long-term damage?"

As she often did when in thought, Molly began to finger one of her braids. "Yeah, hunger's probably the likeliest explanation. As for long-term damage, though, I'd say probably not. You usually see that in famine victims who are really emaciated, which she isn't."

Mrs. Davidson nodded cheerfully. "Well, that's what I thought. Now," she added, rising, "I need to walk over to Ivy Varley's and take her that Amway order she called in last night. By the way, Molly, breakfast was delicious. I do enjoy visiting your Aunt Ruby, but I really missed your cooking. That poor woman can't boil water."

"Well, I enjoy fixing food, and I guess that makes it easier to do a good job of it," Molly said, beaming at the compliment. "Speaking of which, your lunch is in the fridge, Josh."

"Yeah, I need to put in another day at Cranesville, and it's about time I got started." He got up and went to the refrigerator, pausing with his hand on the handle to glance quickly at the front page of the local weekly paper, which Molly had brought in from the porch earlier and laid on the part of the counter that abutted the refrigerator. His nose wrinkled in unconcealed disdain. Above a photo of the gutted armored car, the headline proclaimed:

"VAMPIRE SKELETON STILL
UNACCOUNTED FOR!"

Minutes later, Joshua strode purposefully across the newly-cut lawn behind the house, heading for his shop, a wooden structure facing the alley. Before starting for work, he would need to pick up his tool belt and apron, crow bar, and glass-cutter. Hearing running footsteps in the alley, he glanced up to see his 12-year-old neighbor, Bill "Billy the Kid" Murtaugh, carrying a cat by the tail. "Billy," he called sternly, "How come you're not in school, and what do you think you're doing to that animal?"

"No sweat, man," the buck-toothed boy replied shrilly. "Ain't no school today—teacher's meeting. And this cat's dead—an' I din't kill it, neither. I found it lyin' in the alley a coupla blocks away. Me and Joey Thurman's gonna slit it open so's we can see its guts! He just went to get his dad's guttin' knife."

"Let me guess—you guys just want to get in practice for medical school," Joshua said dryly. The irony in his tone was lost on Billy the Kid.

"Naw, man. We just like to look at guts! It's gonna be totally rad, dude, better'n the movies, even. See ya!"

Shaking his head, Joshua unlocked the shop door's padlock and stepped inside. As he absently gathered up the tools he had come for, he found himself still thinking of Ana. The pained—if he hadn't known better, he would have said terrified—expression on her face the night before still haunted him. Perhaps Molly and his mother were right, and she was suffering from nothing more serious than temporary hunger. But his heart still went out to her with an intensity that surprised him. He was about to put on his tool belt when he heard a car pull up and stop in front of the shop. Setting the things he was carrying down on the workbench, he peered out the window. It wasn't unusual for a customer to bring some wooden object to the shop without calling ahead. What was unusual was that Joshua didn't recognize either the small, white two-door foreign car or the woman who stepped out of it on the driver's side. He reached the still-open shop door just as she did.

"Good morning, ma'am, come on in. What can I do for you?"

"Thank you," was the reply, in a brisk, businesslike voice with a trace of an accent. "I'm looking for a Mr. Joshua Davidson. Have I found him?"

"That you have, though I don't use the 'Mister' part much. I haven't seen you around town before, Miss...?"

"It's Doctor–Dr. Leah Liskowski—and I've never been in Meriwether before last night. I'm a parapsychologist from Northwestern University, near Chicago." As he listened to his visitor speak, Joshua took the opportunity to study her appearance. A slight, somewhat stoop-shouldered woman with dark brown hair pulled into a tight bun, she wore a rather long dress and wire-rimmed glasses. Behind the latter, her hooded eyes were dark and keen-looking. Her unlined face and the absence of any trace of grey in her hair suggested to Joshua that she might be no more than in her forties, but he knew he had never been good at guessing women's ages.

He knit his brows curiously. "I know what a psychologist is, but I'm not familiar with the term you used, Doctor."

The newcomer smiled faintly. "I find that many people aren't." She scratched her hawk-like nose thoughtfully before continuing, as if choosing her words. "Parapsychology is the study of psychic phenomena— what we might define as events or experiences the causes of which are unknown and seemingly inconsistent with presently understood natural laws. I heard about one such event in the news yesterday, and since the university is closed for spring break, I thought I'd drive over here and look into the matter myself. Your local fire chief, a Mr. Cletus Fairbairn, indicated that you might be able to tell me something about it." Realization of what she was talking about suddenly struck Joshua, and his surprise was mixed with irritation.

"Doctor Liskowski," he said, a bit more sharply than he had intended, "the cause of the fire Tuesday night isn't unknown. A drunk driver plowed into the back of another vehicle, and his gas tank exploded. That sort of thing happens all too often."

"Oh, I agree, of course," his caller replied. "The cause of the accident isn't what I find mysterious—it's the total disappearance of a skeleton the armored car was carrying, a skeleton I've read a bit about in the newspapers over the past few weeks, when it was being exhibited in several Eastern cities. It was remarkable primarily because of a very unusual dental peculiarity, which happened to interest me, and now it's missing. Mr. Fairbairn told me you were inside the armored vehicle when the fire was put out. Would you mind giving me an account of what you saw, and letting me tape record it? I can come back this evening, if you're busy now."

Joshua's immediate reaction was that the sooner the woman's questioning was over, the better. Probably it wouldn't delay him much. "Now will be as good a time as any, I think," he said. "Have a seat over here."

Perching on the stool he beckoned her to, the visitor took a battery-operated tape recorder from the shoulder bag she carried, set it on the table beside her, and switched it on. "Tell me in your own words what you found when you entered the burned area," she said. In reasonable detail, without any sensationalism or exaggeration, Joshua proceeded to do so. She listened quietly and, when he had finished, continued to scratch her nose broodingly for a moment or two before shutting off her machine, as if she had only then remembered it.

Steepling her fingers, she looked at Joshua intently. "Mr. Fairbairn's surmise was that the skeleton had simply been burned up, as were many other articles of the cargo. But the skeleton was resting inside a coffin, which was originally lying upright near the rear of the storage compartment, and overturned just beyond the edge of the fire's furthest extent. That area was marked by the charring of the bottom of the coffin, and the near destruction of its lid, which strangely seems to have swung open against the forces of gravity and of the blast from the explosion. The bones were loose, and would have slid in a jumble to the side of the coffin that ended up on the floor, and then spilled out of the top when it opened, on the side away from the fire. If the top of the coffin survived the fire, do you not find it strange that not a single bone was spared, since they would certainly have come to rest in the same area?"

Joshua blinked uneasily. "Yes, but perhaps the force of the blast knocked them away from there," he suggested.

"Perhaps. But in that case, it would seem that their movement would have been away from the blast and therefore away from the fire, not toward it. And it is improbable that an entire skeleton, including the very thick bones of the skull and hips, could be incinerated without trace at a temperature no higher than a mere gasoline explosion can generate. You said that the stake was lying on the side of the coffin away from the fire?"

"Yes, but it wasn't right beside the coffin, either. It was a ways to the left of it."

Leah frowned, clearly trying to visualize the scene in her mind. "Most peculiar, all in all."

Joshua mentally held on to the saving certainty that the impossible, by definition, did not happen. And any activity by genuine vampires obviously fitted into that category. "Doctor, you surely aren't suggesting that a vampire came to life back there and just walked away, are you?" he asked bluntly.

"I don't have enough information to suggest that, nor even to think it. However, vampirism is a particular interest of mine. I've studied it intensively for years...." She broke off, evidently noticing Joshua's disbelieving stare.

"Ma'am, I don't mean to be rude," he said, carefully keeping his tone free of scorn, "But how could anyone study something that everyone knows can't possibly exist?" He feared his directness might have hurt her feelings, but she only smiled slightly.

"I've been asked that question too often to be offended by it. What would you say if I told you that there are any number of cases on record of psychopaths who attacked animals, and sometimes other humans, in order to drink their blood, and that some of these psychopaths display behaviors that folk traditions have associated with vampires? Or that some reputable scholars have theorized that the rare genetic disease porphyria—a lack of red blood pigment—may lead, or in olden times have led, some of its victims to drink human or animal blood, because doing so would temporarily relieve the disease's symptoms? Or that a Vampire Research Center staffed by respectable students of psychic phenomena exists on Long Island, for the serious study of vampiric phenomena, and that its files are at times utilized by police and sheriff's departments all over the country?"

"I'd say it was still a long way between those kinds of things and the sort of things most people mean when they talk about vampires," Joshua said doggedly. Abruptly, he recalled part of his conversation with Ana the evening he had met her. "But maybe you can tell me something. These people with that rare blood disease, who might have drunk blood in the old days—was Count Dracula one of those? Or was he one of those mental cases that act like vampires?"

"Probably neither. His contemporaries didn't accuse him of vampire-like behavior, though they did of just about everything else. He owes that part of his reputation solely to Bram Stoker's use of him as the title character of Dracula. But why do you ask? Most people aren't even aware of the fact that he really lived."

"Oh, I was just curious, because the other day someone who's from Transylvania told me Dracula had been a real person." The parapsychologist darted a piercing glance at him.

"Indeed? And who might that someone have been?"

"Just a young woman hitchhiking across country, whom I happened to meet Tuesday evening. She's staying in an abandoned house a ways outside of town, until she earns some more traveling money. Her name's—let's see if I can pronounce it like she did—Ana Vasil...i...fata."

Leah Liskowski pursed her lips thoughtfully, her expression unreadable. "Could you describe this young lady?" Something in her manner made Joshua vaguely uncomfortable with the question.

"She's about my age and height, with dark hair and eyes, very pretty, and quite pleasant to talk to. Why do you ask?"

"A few years ago, I spent a sabbatical year studying in Romania, and a good part of that time doing field work in Transylvania. I found it a beautiful, fascinating place, and ever since then I've enjoyed meeting people from there. Where is this abandoned house she's staying in?"

"Ah, just go west on Main Street, follow it about a mile out of town to a bend in the road, and you can't miss the place. Now, Doctor, I have a demolition job I need to be going to."

"Of course. I need to be running along myself," she answered. "Thanks so much for your time—you've really been extremely helpful."

As they walked out into the warm sunlight, their ears were abruptly assaulted by raucous cries from Billy Murtaugh and Joey Thurman. Both boys were squatting in the grass across the alley, around the dead cat. The animal's gut cavity had been split open, and a mass of intestines spilled from it.

"Bogus, dude," Joey barked shrilly. "What gives? Ain't no way that can be!"

Joshua and Leah stopped, staring. "What are you two so noisy about?" Joshua called. Turning, Billy held up the animal. There was something strange there....

"Weird, man! This cat ain't got no blood. Not one drop!"

Werner Lind

Chapter Seven

Not for the first time, Ana found herself wishing she had a chair to sit on as she sewed, having risen a while earlier and ascended the cellar stairs to work some more on Joshua's mother's mending. But at least the floor was cleaner than it had been, now that she had brushed away the worst of the dust with a pine bough she had broken off a tree behind the house, and Joshua's lantern was certainly handy, throwing much more light than any candle could. The pillow case she now drew from the bag made her think of goose feathers. In turn, that image evoked a sudden memory, playing itself out once again in her mind....

* * * *

Jolted painfully as the wagon rumbled through the city gates of Brasov, on the other side of Mount Timpa from her home village, Ana stirred and shifted inside the pile of goose feathers that warmed and concealed her. The youngest of eighteen children, with ten older sisters for whom her very poor parents had been obliged to provide dowries, Ana was unmarried at twenty-three. Three separate times she had made the journey to the Maiden's Fair on Gaina Mountain, where the shepherds and goat-herders of her homeland, who spent much of the year in the high mountains with their flocks, took their one annual opportunity to meet marriageable girls and pair off.

Three times she had made the humiliating journey home after being passed over by every prospective groom on the fairgrounds. Too poor, too tall, and too independent-minded, by now Ana seemed destined for lifelong spinsterhood. But something inside her refused to meekly accept the constant hints of pity or contempt in the tone and words with which people addressed her, or the knowledge that she would never nurse a baby nor hear a child call her "Mother," or the lonely nights of wakeful, half-understood desire never finding fulfillment. And now, at last, she had done something about it.

In Brasov, she had heard, there were many young men who owned no flocks to follow, men who worked year-round in the city's shops and countinghouses. A chance to be courted in such a place might at least be more than a once-a-year occurrence. So, having heard that her neighbor Andrei planned to take a load of feathers to Brasov to sell there for pillows, Ana had risen in the wee hours before dawn, slipped out of the small cottage and down the mountainside to Andrei's hovel, and stowed herself away in his wagon. She felt more than slight pangs of guilt at sneaking away in such a fashion, without a good-bye, on a venture her parents would never have permitted, nor Andrei knowingly have cooperated in. Nonetheless, she told herself, what must be, must be. There would be time to send a message to her family once she had found work and lodging in the city. Just now, her first priority would be survival. Winter's snowy grip was tight on the land, and the ragged clothes on her back, which were all she possessed, left much to be desired in terms of warmth.

When the wagon stopped, she heard Andrei asking directions of the passers-by. Swiftly, she raised the tarp at the wagon's back and swung over the tailgate. As soon as her feet touched the cobblestones of the street, she darted into the shadows of the nearest alley and started for its far end, dusting feathers from her clothing as she went. Her first order of business, she told herself, would be to exchange her services at cooking or dishwashing for lodging at an inn.

By about an hour later, Ana was beginning to seriously doubt the wisdom of her venture. Every inn she had approached so far already had a full crew of kitchen servants. The sun had set some time ago. Darkness had fallen and the cold was growing more intense. Despite her jacket, two woolen shawls and doubled stockings, the freezing air raised goose pimples on her chilled flesh. She could no longer feel her toes, and her legs felt like leaden shafts. Moreover, she had not eaten since supper the night before.

Turning a corner, she slipped on a patch of ice and fell full length. Her lifted eyes, as she staggered up, fell on the painted picture of a bear's head on the signboard of the nearest building, another inn. Her decision to try again was the fruit of determination alone, not of any genuine optimism.

Sounds of music and laughter met her ears as she pushed the door open. Inside, some two dozen men and a few women sat either at long trestle tables or in front of the enormous, blazing hearth. Some were eating a late supper; most were just drinking from pewter tankards, and singing a ballad in unison while an old man accompanied them on a tambal. Ana moved toward the fire, almost hypnotized by its warmth. Suddenly, a squat, burly form barred her way. "My fire is for my paying customers, woman," boomed the landlord. "If you are come to buy a meal or lodging, you are welcome here."

Her speech slightly slurred by the numbness of her very cold lips, Ana replied as best she could. "Please, honored sir, for a very small bowl of corn mush and a cup of water, I will wash every dirty dish there be in your house, and clean your kitchen too. Forsooth, I be a very good worker...."

The innkeeper only laughed shortly. "So are the two girls I pay to do such things. If you have no money, get you out and stop dripping on my floor!"

"Prithee, sir," Ana said desperately, "There be a stable here, surely? If I may but sleep in the straw there this night, I know that on the morrow I can find some service to do in payment."

"I keep no almshouse here," bawled the innkeeper. He gestured peremptorily to the tap-boy. "Nicolae, throw her out!"

"A moment, good sir!" a new voice spoke up suddenly. Ana turned to see a powerfully built, well-dressed man, who appeared to be about forty years old, advancing from the small, bare table in one corner where he had been sitting alone. As he came closer, she saw that he was of pale complexion with very dark eyes and hair, and a keen glance with a strangely compelling quality. His voice was very deep and smooth, reminding her of the church organ back in her village. "You offer poor hospitality to such a lovely guest, man!" He looked Ana up and down, rather appraisingly, but as she blushed in awareness of her bedraggled appearance and much-mended clothing, he bowed deeply to her. "Miklos Trina at your service, madam."

Startled by this show of manners, Ana stood blinking a moment or two before remembering her own. "Ana Vasilifata," she replied, making an awkward curtsy on legs which were becoming painful as her circulation renewed in the warmth of the room.

"I am most pleased to meet you. Hast thou not had supper yet? Let me buy you some. Landlord," he said, tossing the man a gold coin from a jewel-studded belt purse, "Bring the lady a bowl of stew with plenty of meat in it, some white bread and sheep's cheese, and a tankard of plum brandy, at my table, and be quick about it. You are cold, madam. Pray come over here and warm yourself at the fire. The wind without is enough to chill the blood."

Whispering her thanks, Ana accepted his offered arm and moved eagerly to the fireside. Hot tears came to her eyes at the pain of returning life in her fingers and toes, but it was worth it. After a few minutes, the welcome warmth had begun to bake the deathlike chill from her body, and to dry the dampness of the snow from her clothing.

Her new companion observed her in silence for a while. "You seem to have traveled some distance this day," he said at last.

"From my home village, Nagy Timpa," she answered shyly. "On the far side of the mountain."

"Ah, yes, a fair part of the country, in truth. I see that our host hath brought your supper at last. Feel you warm enough now to come and eat?"

Ana nodded and let him escort her over to his table, where he drew her chair out for her before seating himself. From long habit, she bowed her head, crossed herself, and mumbled a short grace. Looking up, she raised her eyebrows in alarm. Her benefactor's face had contorted with pain and terror, one hand clutching at his heart as if he'd been stabbed. "Art ill, sir?" she exclaimed, ready to cry for help.

"Oh, nay, nay," he answered, the distortion of his features easing rapidly. "'Twas naught to be fretted about, only a...a passing heart twinge that troubleth me now and again. I be quite well now." He managed a reassuring smile. "Pray you, go ahead and eat."

Thus encouraged, and with her empty stomach already growling like a caged beast, Ana fell to devouring the stew, ravenously putting away spoonful after spoonful until the realization abruptly struck her that Miklos Trina had ordered no food for himself. She felt vaguely abashed to have eaten so greedily in the presence of someone who did not join in the meal. "Come now, sir, are you not hungry?" she said. "Please have some bread and cheese...." She began to break off a piece of the round loaf.

"Please, no," he said quickly. "Worry not about me. I be not hungered just now. I shall have a bite of something anon, perchance. Now, Ana—dost not mind my calling you by your Christian name?—tell me of yourself."

In the next two hours of conversation, Ana did most of the talking, while Miklos plied her with questions and the unaccustomed brandy relaxed her and loosened her tongue. Like most people in her village, Ana usually drank beer with her meals. Plum brandy was a luxury, taken only rarely in small doses added to a cup of hot tea. She had never drunk it straight before, nor in this quantity. But after her long day in the feather wagon without a drink, she was parched with thirst; even the dirty snow and slush of the streets had looked tempting to her dry mouth, and she had refrained only from fear of chilling her insides and freezing to death. Nevertheless, she had refused at first when Miklos had motioned to a servant to refill her tankard but had yielded when he reminded her that the bread was much too dry to eat without dipping it in something. Feeling increasingly warm and comfortable, Ana found herself telling her new friend all about her life, her family and her village, and her reason for coming to Brasov.

Though she made some attempts to get Miklos to talk as freely about himself, she did not succeed. He revealed only that he was a childless widower whose wife had died "some years" earlier, that he lived in an inherited castle some forty miles distant, and that he had traveled to the city on unspecified "business."

At length, having reached a conversational lull long after licking her bowl clean and scooping up and eating her bread and cheese crumbs, Ana looked around and became aware that the room was now darkened and largely empty. The door had been barred, and the windows shuttered. Most of the company had retired to their rooms. A few of the guests, unable to afford beds, had lain down to sleep on the floor in front of the hearth, in which the fire had been banked for the night. Only a single candle still burned, and it was on the far side of the room, where two seedy-looking young men were still rolling dice for money. The brandy she had consumed, Ana realized, was beginning to make her drowsy, though when she spoke she could still do so clearly. "Sir, I thank you with my whole heart for your kindness," she said softly. "It groweth late, and I keep you from your rest." She looked hopefully at the bare floor before the fireplace. "Think you the landlord would care, did I sleep there this night? He hath taken no measures to hinder it."

Miklos smiled wryly, amused at some thought Ana did not catch. "Methinks he rather expected you would sleep in another place, Ana," he said after a pause, during which he eyed her as if he were considering something. "But howsoever that be, your clothing be surely too damp to sleep in, and the floor be hard and unrestful. Needs must you sleep in a real bed, with a soft mattress and warm blankets—like the bed in my room."

"Oh, nay, sir," Ana replied instantly. "I have imposed too far upon you already. I'll not put you out of your own bed."

"Sooth," he said quietly, meeting her eyes with his intense gaze, "'twas my thought that we might share it." As he spoke, he laid his right hand softly on her left where she rested it on the table.

At that moment, Ana was in the act of swallowing the last of her brandy. When the full import of his meaning registered in her mind, she choked so violently that she sent drops of liquid clean across the table, causing the dice players to dart momentary curious glances at her. "Art well?" Miklos said with quick solicitude.

"Y-yea... I mean, nay. That is, I, I did swallow the wrong way," she stammered, feeling herself blush to the roots of her hair. She was shocked by Miklos' offer, but more deeply by the realization that part of her found it tempting. Her thoughts seemed to be revolving like the aksak rhythm of an invirtita dance—now this way, now that, now halting, now moving. Miklos had no living wife, nor did she have a husband. But she would have a husband, no matter what everyone else said, and she would not soil what she kept in trust for him, not even if she drank a lake full of brandy! And besides, she called herself a Christian, not a heathen Turk; should not the Church's law mean something to her? She gripped the table edge, picturing the icons on the wall of the hut she had grown up in, recalling the taste of the bread in her mouth at Mass. After straightening and taking a deep breath, she managed to answer without a noticeable tremor in her voice. "Sir, I be grateful for all your kindness to me, but I cannot do what you suggest. You and I be not lawfully wed."

"That be remediable, in truth," he said simply, not taking his hand from hers. She felt her eyes widen as he continued. "Ana, you please me; to have you about me all the time is a most fair prospect. So, if so be that you consent, I would fain make you my bride. 'Tis hardly the hour of the night to summon a priest, but unless I know not the canon law, an engagement duly pledged be no less binding than the wedding ceremony itself." He removed one of several jeweled rings he wore, and laid it in her hand. "Wilt accept this in pledge of my troth?"

Any facade of self-control Ana had been able to muster had collapsed during this speech. Her confusion and indecision, she realized, must be evident now in every aspect of her bearing and expression. As Miklos closed them over the ring, her fingers were trembling. Could this conversation be real, or was it a weird dream? That a man might propose marriage to a woman he had met only a few hours before did not strike her as odd in itself. At the Maiden's Fair, betrothals were often made on the basis of much less conversation than she and Miklos had already had, and some couples whose engagements were made by their families met for the first time at their own weddings. But that this man, who was obviously of high birth and considerable wealth, might seriously propose marriage to a woman of her lowly station and circumstances struck her as more than odd— it was unbelievable. True, she had come here for no other reason than to find a husband, but she had expected that enterprise to take months, not hours, and to result in a union with a merchant's clerk or a craftsman's journeyman, not with the master of Castle Trina!

She rubbed her free hand across her face, aware that the liquor in her belly was making it harder for her to think. "Sir," she said weakly, "you mock me in a manner unworthy of a gentleman. You know we be not of equal station, and that I can bring you no dowry of any worth in your eyes."

Her suitor shook his head earnestly and leaned forward, speaking in a persuasive tone. "I am so circumstanced that I need care nothing for the payment of a dowry, Ana. And in truth, I deem most young maidens of my own rank to be colorless and boring. I canst choose what bride I please, and I am well pleased to choose you. I protest and swear, I have no mind whatever to bed you and leave you. Come you to my room now, you come as my rightful betrothed, with my pledge in your hand, and we shall belong to each other always." He paused a moment. "You came hither seeking a husband. Am I so poor a prospect that you must disdain me?"

As she listened, Ana's thoughts were a confused jumble of elation and distrust, gratitude and fear, desire and hesitation. His final appeal pushed her over the brink on which she had been teetering. Not trusting herself to speak, she simply put the offered ring in her pocket, and placed her right hand in his.

He rose immediately and helped her to her feet. Her gait slightly unsteady, she leaned heavily on his arm. She found herself at his door, scarcely able to remember the steps by which she had gotten there.

Having unlocked the door with a key, he motioned her, with a bow, to precede him. Stumbling into the room, she found it pitch-dark. Evidently the windows were shuttered or curtained very tightly, for no light at all shone in from the street or sky. She heard Miklos lock the door behind him. "Sir, where...where be the bed?" she mumbled, while vainly trying to pierce the gloom by squinting. His answering voice came from a pace or two behind her. The smooth tones held a strange note she couldn't quite interpret.

"'Tis across the room, in the corner. Let me guide you," he added, turning her slightly and taking her arm.

A few strides brought her probing fingers, held in front of her, into contact with a lidded wooden box, evidently part of Miklos' luggage. "We did take a wrong turn in this dark," she whispered thickly. "This be not a bed."

"Oh, but it is," her betrothed answered, again with that strange note in his voice. She turned and tried to discern his facial expression through the blackness. "Needs must my bed be out of common—as yours will be henceforth. I shall indeed make you my bride, but that status doth carry a certain condition which I mentioned not, heretofor."

The next thing she knew, his hand had clamped over her mouth with a force she would not have believed possible, and then his teeth buried themselves in her neck.

* * * *

With a start, Ana came from the remembered past to the tangible present, abruptly recalling where she was.

Then she felt her tears begin to flow, slowly dropping, one by one, onto the forgotten pillowcase in her lap.

Werner Lind

Chapter Eight

As noon drew near the next day, Joshua stolidly piled chunk after chunk of broken plaster into the wheelbarrow. With the roof of the former hatchery now gone, and one wall removed, unseasonably hot sunlight beat down into the structure's shell. Joshua's T-shirt was soggy with sweat. He reached up absently, for the hundredth time, to wipe his face. His task was a familiar and mechanical one, requiring no really attentive thought, and all morning his mind had wandered between two subjects.

The one that occupied him now was the strange matter of the dead cat which had turned up the day before. He'd reported the incident to Tom, and the two men had gone together to the local veterinarian, Doc Walsh, enjoining him and his nurse, Pansy Truett, to silence about the matter. They had not wished to create a panic—although there was little chance, Joshua thought grimly, that something like this could really be kept quiet. Doc had been as baffled as the two younger men, avowing that he knew of no blood disease that would cause a total disappearance of the victim's blood, or produce the two puncture-like lesions on the animal's throat which his examination had disclosed. Perhaps Tom was correct in thinking that a vampire bat, possibly escaped from a zoo, had been responsible.

Thoughts of Ana—the second recurrent subject of his attention—sifted back into Joshua's mind. Awake or asleep, images of Ana's face and hair, and especially of her sad, gentle eyes, kept returning to him. He'd never before been always thinking about a girl, nor could he recall ever having dreamt of one—though, to be sure, his high school psych teacher had said that people forget the majority of their dreams. Not that he hadn't dated as much as most young men. One of his high school classmates had once remarked that all her friends wanted to date him, because he was good-looking, good company, and kept his hands where they belonged. Each young woman he had gone out with had had something attractive in her personality, and some were very pretty in face and form as well. Yet none of them had ever begun to affect him the way this stranger did. Was it, he wondered, her very strangeness—the exotic quality of her foreignness and sense of mystery—that drew his attention so? Or was it something much deeper, something in the soul looking out of her dark eyes that called to his own? In any case, he reflected, shaking his head decisively and thrusting his handkerchief back into his pocket, however ironic the fact might be, Ana was the one woman it would not be wise to lose his head, or his heart, over. She was not going to stay in Meriwether any longer than it took to raise the money to move on, nor had she shown any sign of returning his interest, or of even wanting to let him get to know much about her.

He seized the handles of the heavily-loaded wheelbarrow and, muscles knotting, shoved it through the gap where the hatchery's doors had been and out across the trodden-to-death turf to his pickup. A glance at his watch told him it was now noon. Raising his eyes to where the walls of the new store were rising, he saw Tim O'Connor motion to him. The red-haired journeyman was already seated on the ground with his brown bag in his lap.

After getting his own lunch pail from the truck cab, Joshua walked over and joined the forming circle, seating himself on a cinder block beside Tim. Jigger, back on the job today, his eyes bloodshot and his expression sour, plunked his rather large bulk down on Joshua's other side. Looking up after he finished his grace, the young carpenter saw Wade start toward the group, but the older man stopped abruptly on the near side of the cement mixer, looking down disgustedly at one foot. He vented a couple of angry curses, then looked a trifle abashed as he saw Joshua silently wince. "Pardon my French, Josh," he grunted.

"What happened?"

"Aw, I stepped down in a mess of dog poop. I wish the clod-hoppin' morons down here would tie up their mangy curs."

"Might notta been anybody's pet dog," Tim interjected with the equanimity of someone whose shoes had luckily avoided the pile. "Mighta been one of those wild dogs that've been runnin' around all over the county. My old man was sayin' the supervisors oughta get off their rears and appoint an animal warden."

Wade snarled voicelessly, then wiped his shoe on what little grass he could find. "Well, they better do something," he grumbled. Stalking over to the board supported on bricks where Itchy and Bull sat, he cuffed his son on the shoulder. "Move your butt."

"I'm glad to see you're feeling better today, Itchy," Joshua said politely.

Itchy, who'd missed work the day before and whose nose sported a discolored bruise, snorted and glared at his questioner. "Yeah, I bet you are," he said. "What ya wearin' a shirt for in this heat? Afraid some of the women down here'll see your chest?"

"Oh, I wouldn't want to distract them from yours, Itchy."

Jigger spoke up, peering curiously at Itchy's bare torso. "Speakin' of your chest, Itchy, what in Sam Hill ya got around your neck? Ya get religion or somethin'?" Looking more closely, Joshua realized that his former classmate had hung what appeared to be a pair of popsicle sticks, tied in the shape of a cross, around his neck with a length of binder twine.

"'Course not," Itchy spat. "Why would I get religion? Do I look like some kind of kook?" He jerked slightly as his father kicked his leg.

"It wouldn't hurt you to get a little religion," Wade growled. "You could stand some improvement."

"I got a feelin' I shouldn't ask," Tim said before Itchy could reply, "but then why have you got a cross hangin' on your neck?"

"All right, I'll tell ya why," Itchy declared self-importantly. "It's to proteck me from the vampire we got runnin' around here." As the other five men stared at him, he added defiantly, "Well, ain't you heard about that cat they found with all the blood sucked outta it, and two holes in its neck? Ellie Murtaugh told my ma all about it last night at bingo over at St. Mary's."

"Well, I heard all about it from Pansy Truett's husband at Callan's last night," Tim answered. "But the way I heard it, it was probably a vampire bat that got loose from a zoo, not Dracula the Second."

So much for Tom's hope of keeping any of this quiet, Joshua thought disgustedly. Aloud, he said dryly, "Why didn't they just put this in the paper?"

"'Cause this week's paper was printed up already," Bull answered patiently, with the air of one obliged to explain the obvious. "Old Man Rhodes' printer told my cousin they might print an extra, though," he added.

"Anyway, it wasn't a vampire that did it—get that through your dumb, thick head, ya idiot," Wade roared abruptly at his son. "Even in them crazy movies ya waste your money on, did ya ever see a vampire bite a cat? If there was any vampires—and there ain't—they ain't supposed to suck blood outta cats; they're supposed to suck it outta good-lookin' women."

"A cat today, maybe a woman tomorrow," Itchy retorted. He scraped the remains of peanut butter and bread from his back teeth with one finger before continuing. "Anyway, I know more about this than that jackass sheriff does. I got me a pretty good idea of who the vampire is—I think I seen her already."

Itchy's choice of pronoun suddenly registered in Joshua's mind. "Just who are you talking about, Itchy?" he said sharply.

"I seen this big tall broad with black hair, that's real pale and wears a big black cape with a high collar that sticks up behind her head, like all them vampires wear, and she talks with a vampire accent, just like in the movies. I, uh, I passed her in an alley, when I was out for a walk 'cause I couldn't sleep."

"Was that the night before last, when ya fell on your nose and came home bitchin' about a king-sized bellyache and stayed home from work the next day?" Wade said with a snort.

"Yeah, but never mind that," Itchy snapped. "You can bet it was her that bit that cat."

Joshua felt a hot flush of anger surging over his face and neck. "Itchy, I've met the young lady you're talking about—"

"Oh yeah? And where'd ya meet up with her, Mister Holier-Than-Thou?"

"I'm not going to dignify a question in that tone with an answer," Joshua said, aware that there was an edge to his voice and not caring. "But I will explain this to you— once. The lady happens to be pale because she's been hitchhiking a long way and hasn't had much money for food. She's from...Eastern Europe, so she has an accent, and I would imagine she dresses the same way all the other young women over there dress. There's nothing at all—"

Itchy broke in with triumphant delight. "I told ya! That proves it. She's from Eastern Europe. That's where them vampires is always from—them wop countries!"

Tim suddenly burst out laughing. "Oh, yeah, that's real smart, Itchy," he managed through his giggles. "Anybody from Eastern Europe's a vampire! That exchange student at the high school last year was probably one, too. I guess all his classmates shoulda hung Popsicle sticks around their necks, too!"

His sallow face twitching, Itchy stood up and slammed his lunch pail to the ground with an obscenity. "A lot you know! If she's just an ordinary skirt, why's she so stro...aw, forget it; I don't hafta talk to ya. I gotta use the john anyway. Just mark my words—she ain't gonna get any of my blood!" He wheeled and stalked off.

"That kid of mine, he don't know nuthin'. He ain't got the brains God give a flea," Wade grunted. Joshua hardly heard the words. He stared after Itchy, disturbingly aware of a sudden, very real fear for Ana's safety and vaguely aware of another fear that he couldn't put a name to. It certainly wasn't of vampires, since he knew perfectly well that there weren't any—didn't he?

* * * *

Hours later, as he drove down the dirt road that led back into town from the landfill, where he had disposed of a second load of plaster, the feeling of fear still nagged at him. Leah Liskowski had shown a good deal of interest in the dead cat, he recalled as he braked on the outskirts of town. And she had spoken of psychopaths who acted out aspects of the vampire legend and attacked animals, or even people, for their blood. But he recalled Ana's eyes and voice, and knew there was no way that she was a psychopath. And as for the other idea lurking in the background—the preposterous niggling suggestion that the old legend might contain some truth—that had to be on a par with belief in Santa Claus or the tooth fairy; he would stake his life on that. The thought abruptly crossed his mind that he might already have done so—and his mother's and sister's lives as well. Despite the unusual heat, a sudden cold shiver went down his back.

As he approached the corner of Main and Arthur, he saw the grey stone walls of Lewis County's public library, the big maple trees around it casting long shadows in the late afternoon sun. On an impulse, he cut the wheel around and came to a stop in one of the parking slots behind the building. He went around to the front, climbed the crumbling steps, and pushed open the glass door beside the plaque that stated, "BUILT IN 1899, THROUGH THE GENEROSITY OF ANDREW CARNEGIE." Inside the familiar main room, with its walls of bookshelves and the great hearth in one corner, the coolness of the air conditioning was more than welcome. Making his way to the small reference area beside the big, dark wooden counter, he selected the U-V volume of one of the encyclopedia sets, took a chair at the table, and opened the book. It did not take long to find the entry he sought.

"VAMPIRES," he read silently. *"In European, particularly Balkan, folklore, mythical beings*

thought to be animated corpses surviving perpetually without decay, and sustained by the consumption of fresh blood (generally human blood). Humans who die at the hands of a vampire through exsanguination are, in most forms of the superstition, thought to become vampires themselves. Vampires are, according to legend, active only at night, spending the day hidden from sunlight, contact with which would be instantly fatal to them. Other common features of the myth are the vampire's inability to cross a threshold or a windowsill unless invited in; the ascription to the vampire of superhuman strength, said to be equal to that of twenty men; his or her power to telepathically command the obedience of wolves and rats, and to physically transform into a cloud of mist, a wolf, or a bat, while retaining human cunning."

Unbidden, a sudden sharp memory flared in Joshua's mind of Jigger's drunken rantings at the accident scene: "...and then I saw thish bat fly—fly over me and fly away.... It wash a very big bat...." Frowning, Joshua shook his head and read on.

"The folklore of vampires describes them as resembling human beings, but as of very pale complexions and with a hyper-development of the canine teeth into functional fangs; as not casting a reflection in a mirror; and as having a mortal terror of certain Christian religious objects, such

as Communion wafers, holy water, and especially the sign of the cross."

Suddenly, he recalled that his mother had been wearing her cross necklace the night before last—the night Ana had looked so...frightened?

> *"To destroy a vampire, folk beliefs prescribe burning, shooting or stabbing with a silver bullet or knife; or, most commonly, driving a stake through the vampire's heart. However, if the latter method were employed, it was thought that (unless the head had previously been severed) the vampire would be revived if the stake were to be removed from the corpse or skeleton."*

Again, Joshua saw in his mind's eye the bloodstained stake where it had lain in the armored car, beside the charred coffin. Instead of feeling comfortable, for a moment the air-conditioned room felt icy cold.

Biting his lip as he weighed the chain of strange coincidences, he raised his eyes to the front window. Sunlight streamed down outside in golden profusion, shining on the chrome of parked cars on Main Street. Robins ran, chirping, over the library lawn. Across the street, people came and went along the sidewalk in front of the Farm Bureau Co-op Dairy and the Meriwether Hardware Store on the corner. A dusty cattle truck rolled by, the steers inside scratching their hairy sides against the slats. With a deep breath, Joshua relaxed suddenly, brought back to common sense by the sheer weight of the everyday world's familiarity. After all, this was not a B-grade horror flick. This was *reality*: actual life, in a universe where fantasy, by definition, would always be make-believe, nothing more. Whatever chains of coincidence might occur, the impossible would always be impossible. He knew that as well as he knew his own Social Security number, or the routine order of the days of the week.

With a thump, Joshua closed the book before him, and then returned it to its shelf. If he didn't hurry home, he'd be late for supper. A quick drink at the water fountain, a cheery wave to the old librarian, Mr. Peedy, and he was on his way out the door, his mood much lighter than it had been moments ago.

Werner Lind

Chapter Nine

A waxing moon, white against the darkening blue of the evening sky, shone down with a quiet beauty. Seated with her sewing on the ruined house's front porch steps, Ana looked up to admire it for a long moment. She had carried the brown paper bag and Joshua's lantern outside a short while ago, going through the breach in the wall and around the corner of the house, to enjoy the evening while she worked. As she bent to look again at the cuff button which she was sewing back onto a shirt, she heard the characteristic sound of a self-propelled vehicle coming from the direction of Meriwether. Since two or three other vehicles had passed earlier, the approach of another aroused no great interest. But as it came into view it slowed perceptibly, and she recognized it as Joshua's.

"Good morrow, Joshua! Welcome," she called, as he came to a stop at the foot of the path and waved to her. He stepped from the vehicle's enclosure and quickly crossed the short distance between them.

"Hi, Ana. You're working on Mom's mending, I see. How's it going?"

Ana shrugged. "It goeth well enough, I think. But if I match the color of thread to cloth, there be not much more I can sew for now. I have no other spools save these three. Know you of any place where I canst buy some more and mayhap a scissors also? I have been breaking off the thread, but that frayeth the ends somewhat."

"Well, the closest place would probably be the Jones Brothers' General Store, on Main Street in Meriwether. They sell just about everything under the sun. Of course, they charge more than the stores in the bigger cities but not much more. If you want," he added, "I could give you a ride into town to shop—the general store stays open 'til around nine o'clock."

Ana considered the offer briefly but did not yet feel ready to trust herself to his strange vehicle. Traveling on foot might be slower, but it would get her there undamaged. "Nay, I'll go another time, Joshua, but I thank you. Come now, what errand hath brought you hither—and what have you there?" she added, gesturing to a fairly thick roll of folded paper he had in one hand. Its surface seemed to be covered with printed script from a press, like the handbills she had seen at times in London.

"Oh, I just came out to pick up whatever mending you might have done so far. And this is a copy of yesterday's Herald—that's our weekly newspaper. I thought you might like to read the want ads to see if there are any advertisements for work you could do."

At this last statement, Ana bent her head to the mending bag beside her, letting her long, hanging locks cloak her sudden embarrassment. "Here be the things I have mended as yet," she answered, passing them to Joshua one by one as she separated them from the articles still undone. He put them into a white bag of some unknown material, which he pulled from his back pocket. "As to the other, 'twas a kind thought, Joshua, but a vain one, I fear. I cannot read so much as one word upon that page." Glancing over at him, she saw his brows rise in evident surprise, which suddenly vanished in an understanding grin.

"Of course," he exclaimed. "They don't use this alphabet in your country, do they? You're used to that—what do they call it—Cyrillic alphabet, like they use in Russia. I've seen things written in that, on television. Would you like to learn to read and write in English? I'll be glad to teach you." Ana felt her eyes widen with surprise and pleasure. That such an offer might be made had been the furthest possibility from her mind, but she was instantly aware of the practical benefits such attainments of learning might confer. Almost as quickly, however, she was assailed by doubt. "Though 'twould be a great boon to me, Joshua," she said cautiously, "think you that I could learn, in the short time that I shall abide here? And besides," she added, dropping her gaze and feeling unaccountably embarrassed, "Such teaching would make too great a claim upon your time."

"No, it wouldn't," was the prompt reply. "I can't think of anything I'd enjoy doing more, and why shouldn't I spend time on something I enjoy? And as far as your being able to learn, you strike me as a quick learner, Ana. You've already learned to speak English without being taught it, and that shows a smart mind. Most people couldn't just pick up a foreign language and speak it as well as you do. With somebody to teach you, I'd say that in a few weeks, you'll be able to read English as well as you read Romanian now." *I can do that already,* Ana thought wryly, quirking one eyebrow.

But his words were persuasive. "Then, Joshua," she said, raising her head, "I shall be your pupil right willingly. When wish you to begin?"

He smiled. "That's the spirit! I'd say there's no time like the present. We can use the newspaper, for starters, and I'll bring some paper and pencils the next time I come." He spread the newspaper, motioning Ana to move closer so they could share it, and adjusted his position to the lantern. "In our alphabet, we have twenty-six letters, starting with A. That letter's a small A, and that one is what we call a capital A, but the sound's the same."

Caught up in the wonder of the secrets which soon began to be unlocked to her, Ana lost track of time. To her, reading was a virtually magical art, a precious and mighty knowledge far above the ken of ordinary people. She had never known anyone who could do it, except the priest in her village, and his ability had been a part of his supernatural aura. And now she was reading—for at the end of the evening's lesson, she actually read, though slowly and stumblingly, a short sentence!

Joshua beamed, nearly as pleased with her achievement as she was. "Way to go! Do you realize, you've only had one short lesson, and you've already read your first sentence in English? What did I tell you?"

Ana beamed herself but gestured self-deprecatingly. "The merit is yours, you are a good teacher. When canst thou come again?"

Joshua's reply was unhesitating. "I should be able to come tomorrow evening. I'd come during the day, but a friend of mine and I already made plans to spend the day fishing, and then he's coming to supper. But after that he's taking my sister to the drive-in, and I'll be free. If you like, I'll leave the paper here. You can practice reading in it, and then show me what you've been able to read without help." He glanced down at the newspaper, frowning abruptly, then looked up to meet her questioning eyes. "That reminds me—have you had a visit yesterday or today from a Dr. Leah Liskowski?"

Ana shook her head, instantly curious. "Nay—should I have?"

"I expect you will before long." Heaving a deep sigh, he went on to relate his entire earlier conversation with Dr. Liskowski. Ana listened with increasing concern and dismay, reflected in the restless movements of her hands in her lap.

When he finished, she remained silent for a moment. "If this woman would speak to me of my homeland," she said finally, "She is welcome to do so, though I have been away from home for many years and mayhap can say but little that would interest her. Twould seem that she meaneth no harm."

"No, but I can't say the same for a guy I know, who's also taking some interest in you, apparently—a fellow by the name of Itchy Bruggenhorst." Hearing the name, Ana started, a reaction that did not escape Joshua's notice. "You recognize his name?"

She nodded. "I did cross his path in Meriwether two nights agone—I had gone thither to see the town," she added tersely. "But tell me of him, and his...interest."

Again, Joshua launched into a narrative, this time of Itchy's statements at lunch earlier that day. The disquiet his information about Dr. Liskowski had produced was mild alongside the icy touch of real fear that his new revelation evoked. After he had finished, she remained silent again, not so much in thought this time as out of unwillingness to speak until she could make her voice appear casual.

Joshua spoke before she did. "I didn't mean to scare you or upset you by telling you this, Ana, but I thought you ought to know. Nobody around here except Itchy would come up with such a crazy idea, or believe it, either. But he's foolish enough to actually believe it, and he's got a real mean streak that makes him dangerous. I don't mind telling you, I worry about you being out here all alone."

"Prithee, worry not," she said firmly, with an outward confidence she was far from feeling inside. "I can protect myself from his ilk. And look you, Joshua," she added, inspired by a sudden encouraging thought, "He knows not where I bide. Even if he would, he couldst not find me to do harm."

"That's true, I guess," Joshua agreed. "But listen, if you want to go to town again, promise you'll let me take you. There's no sense running into him alone again. Hey—did he try to hurt you the other night?"

"He did me no harm, as you canst see," she answered quickly and, as far as it went, truthfully. "And I'll not go into the town again until I see you on the morrow. Doth that comfort your worry?" she added in a jesting tone.

He managed an answering smile. "Yes, for now. And now," he concluded, glancing at his watch—which he wore, not chained to his pocket, but rather on his wrist like a bracelet—"it's getting late. I should be heading on home. But I'll look forward to seeing you...uh, to our reading lesson, that is, tomorrow."

"As shall I. Good night, Joshua, and thanks to you."

"You're welcome." He clasped her hand in parting, turned, and made his way to his vehicle. They exchanged a wave as he turned it before heading off in the direction of his home.

Ana watched until the corner of the house cut off her sight of the blue horseless wagon. Many thoughts and sensations vied for her attention, but she was startled at the one she found uppermost—the disturbing consciousness of how attractive Joshua was, not merely in looks, but, more importantly, in personality. And that he felt some attraction to her as well was clear in his eyes and manner and his seeking of reasons to spend time with her. Yet if he knew her secret, any feeling of attraction toward her would surely turn into loathing and disgust. That thought left a cold emptiness in the pit of her stomach. Perhaps it was no kindness to either of them to accept his instruction in reading. It could only throw them more together and increase the pain of the inevitable, and not long to be postponed, parting. But still, it was most worthwhile to learn to read, and surely, surely that chance should be seized upon...ought it not?

Absorbed in these reflections, she had not heard the approach of another vehicle and was startled into awareness when it stopped at the foot of the path. Unlike Joshua's, this conveyance was white, as well as smaller and completely enclosed. A dark-haired, bespectacled woman of indeterminate age, clad in a decent dress and with a bag of some sort strapped over her shoulder, got out and hailed Ana briskly. "Good evening! Might your name be Ana Vasilifata?"

"It is. You have the advantage of me, madam," Ana called in response, though from Joshua's earlier description, she had already guessed her new visitor's identity. The woman's next words confirmed the guess.

"I'm Dr. Leah Liskowski, of Northwestern University," she said, striding up the path without waiting for an invitation. Reaching the steps, she extended her hand. Prepared by Joshua's narrative, Ana returned the other's strong clasp without any show of surprise. Otherwise, the designation "Doctor" would have raised her brows very quickly. *However*, she reflected, *if in this time and place some women wear pants like men, it is perhaps not to be wondered at that a woman might be a doctor in a university.*
"To what owe I your visit, Doctor?" she asked.

"I'm in Meriwether for a few days investigating a matter of possible interest to my field of study, and when I learned where you were from, I became interested in meeting you. A few years ago, I spent a good bit of time studying in Transylvania, so I always enjoy meeting and talking with anyone from that region."

Ana moistened dry lips. "Pray sit you down on the step, then, Doctor, and speak with me whilst I sew. Tis pleasanter out here in the air, with the beauty of the land about us, than 'tis in the dank, mildewed house," she added.

"Oh, I couldn't agree more," the newcomer said, seating herself. Ana did likewise, and took up her needle again. "You aren't an easy person to see. I'd meant to visit you yesterday but was detained by some unexpected interviews I had to do for my research. But when I stopped by here this afternoon, I didn't find you anywhere around."

"Nay, I was...out walking in yonder fields for much of the day. So then, Joshua has told me somewhat of your studies, Doctor."

"Ah, I thought I saw his truck coming back towards town a few minutes ago. Then you know I'm interested in the recent armored car accident near here and in the dead cat that was found in town yesterday as well. Vampirism is a special interest of mine. In fact it was that interest which brought me to Romania. I took some graduate courses in Romanian folklore at the University of Bucharest and did field work in Transylvania. What brought you to America, by the way, if you don't mind my asking?"

"A ship," Ana answered simply.

"Ah, yes. I meant, what caused you to leave your homeland and come here?"

By now, Ana had become very attentive, at least outwardly, to her sewing. "Naught but the wish to travel and see something of the world. There be great pleasure in seeing strange lands and peoples. Have you not found it so, Doctor?"

"Oh, yes, indeed." The learned woman stared intently at her, thoughtfully scratching her own nose. Its shape vaguely reminded Ana of an eagle's beak, and she could almost picture this woman tearing into her with beak and talons as an eagle would into a rabbit or a cony. "Has anyone ever told you that you speak English with a very archaic flavor?"

Ana had no idea what "archaic' might mean but chose not to ask. "Nay, but I thank you for doing so. I learnt the tongue in England, where it be spoken somewhat differently than 'tis here, I find." At these words, she detected a sudden quickening of the doctor's already hawk-like scrutiny, but a moment later it was masked behind a disarming smile.

"Of course. Tell me, Ana, what part of Transylvania are you from?"

"My home village is called Nagy Timpa."

Her visitor nodded. "I know in a general way where that is, but I never did any field work in that locality. So perhaps you can tell me: do any of the older people there, or any of the younger ones, for that matter, still believe in what they call the 'Undead'?"

Nervously, Ana shifted her position on the warped wooden step. "What other folk may believe or not believe, I know not. For myself, I would say this: I think the study of the Undead be a dangerous one for any mortal to follow. Were I you, 'twould not be a matter anyone could pay me to mix in."

Leah Liskowski continued to stare at her, her expression unreadable. "Well, I have studied it for some years, now," she said after a pause, "and I'm none the worse for it. Of course, people in Transylvania often gave me tips on how to protect myself against the 'Undead.' One old gentleman even gave me a wooden crucifix he'd carved himself for that purpose. Although I'm Jewish, I was so touched by his kindness that I've kept the object ever since. In fact, I carry it in my shoulder bag," she added, undoing the clasp as she darted a glance at Ana which seemed to pierce her very soul down to its undergarments. "Let me show it to you—the workmanship is quite exquisite."

Ana rose with a speed she could not have exceeded if she had been propelled by a bullet. "Nay, nay, another time mayhap. I, I cannot tarry longer...there be an errand I must do. F-Fare you well." She managed to utter these words as she backed away from the porch. Then, unable to escape by the obvious route of the front door, she turned and ran full-tilt around the corner of the house toward the gaping orifice in the wall. Even once inside the empty ruin, she could still sense the intensity of the woman's stare, boring into the wall outside as if it could drill through rotting wood and crumbling plaster to peer squarely into Ana's terrified eyes.

Werner Lind

Chapter Ten

Joshua rubbed his eyes as Tom turned the ignition key to silence the low hum of the car's engine. To the east, just above the horizon, the sky showed signs of light. Where they had parked, however, in the shade of a great crab-apple tree that overhung the electric fence to their left, it was still as dark as midnight. The moon had long since set. Turning to his companion, Joshua continued the conversation that had been going on when they had pulled off the dirt road. "What makes you think it wasn't a vampire bat after all?" he asked earnestly.

Tom scratched his moustache before answering. "Well, mostly what that doctor lady from Chicago said. She came by the courthouse Thursday afternoon to question Jigger, before he made bail. Of course, he couldn't remember anything. She questioned Walter and me, too, had us talk into that tape recorder she's got. Anyway, she says vampire bats aren't big enough to suck all the blood out of a full-grown cat. Accordin' to her, the biggest they get is about three, three-and-a-half inches long, and maybe an ounce or two in weight, and most of 'em are smaller. Oh, and she says their teeth aren't as far apart as those puncture wounds were. Their whole heads aren't much wider. And anyway, they don't make puncture wounds and suck blood, they make cuts and lick the blood as it runs."

As he spoke, the two young men stepped out of the front seat, and, from the trunk, gathered their fishing rods, lunch pails, bait cans, and the pail that would hold their catch. Tom continued as they made their way to the gate of the sheep pasture that belonged to Ben Greenlaw, Tom's mother's cousin. "She seemed to know what she was talkin' about. Besides, I've heard from a few of the zoos I contacted. Not one of 'em ever had any bats escape, let alone vampire bats. Besides, they're all so far away, an escaped bat couldn't have waited 'til it got here to eat, but no other sheriff's department in this part of the state has had any reports of similar animal deaths—I've been on the phone to quite a few of 'em. Nope, that explanation sounded good at the time, but I reckon it won't hold water."

Having reached the gate, Tom seized the latch by its sheath of red plastic, opened it, and re-latched it behind them. They struck out across the grass toward the wall of trees and brush half a mile distant which marked the winding course of Clay Creek. From the flock at the far end of the pasture, to their right, a soft bleat from the first ewe to awaken reached their ears. "If a bat didn't attack that cat, what did?" Joshua said, stepping carefully to avoid scattered manure. He looked up, searching his friend's face as well as the darkness would allow, when the lawman hesitated in replying.

"Doc Walsh said it wasn't killed by any disease known to veterinary science, and the boys from Iowa State over at Ames say the same thing. About the only explanation that makes sense to me is that somebody deliberately punctured the animal's neck with a sharp instrument and drained the blood out somehow. That lady parapsychologist, or whatever she calls herself, said there are nut cases runnin' around that have been known to do stuff like that—people who think they're vampires, like the ones in the horror movies. Since we've never had anything like this happen around here before, my guess is it's not somebody local. More likely it's somebody passin' through."

Joshua paused, nervously shifting his grip on the pail. "But you don't know that, Tom. We don't know how many cats or other animals may have been killed around here for years, and just none of the bodies ever discovered."

Tom paused in his tracks for a moment, considering. "Yeah, that's a point," he admitted. "And this Doctor What's-Her-Face did say that if there was somebody local who had a tendency that way—what she called a 'latent delusion', or somesuch thing—but hadn't ever done anything about it, this accident with the armored car, and the way the press played it up, might have been enough to push him over the brink." With sudden anger, he kicked savagely at a loose rock in front of him. "I could about throttle Rhodes over at the Herald. He started this crap. And if Pansy wasn't a woman, I could throttle her, too. I know doggone well she's the one that ran her big mouth off about this thing with the cat. And now Rhodes has brought out his extra, and put this out to the wire services, and Herman Towers says that a reporter from the National Tattler made a reservation at the motel. Heaven knows where it'll all end."

"The National Tattler?" Joshua exclaimed in dismay. "Oh, no. Isn't that one of those junky tabloids they sell at the supermarket, with stories about two-headed babies and people being abducted by space aliens? They're going to write about Meriwether?"

Tom nodded grimly. "Yeah, I thought it was pretty doggone disgustin' myself," he said, his tone reflecting his statement.

"Were there any likely suspects on Mr. Towers' register?" Joshua said after a moment's pause, having guessed Tom's likeliest reason for talking to the owner of the Shady Lodge Motel.

"No. It was mostly just the usual motorists that happened to be travelin' through here Wednesday night when they got tired, and a sales rep that's stayed there several times before—he sells to the variety store. Only folks that weren't checked out by noon on Thursday were that doctor lady and an insurance investigator who works for the company that insured all that stuff on the armored car. 'Course, even if whoever we're dealin' with isn't from around here, that doesn't mean he, or she, checked into the motel. Drifters and hitchhikers pass through every now and then and sleep outside, or in barns or wherever else they can find." The sheriff fell silent for a while, lifting his fishing pole to rest it on his shoulder.

When he spoke again, it was with a casualness that somehow did not come across as convincing. "That doctor tells me you ran into a transient when you were comin' home from the fire—young woman that says she from Transylvania, I believe?"

Joshua followed the drift of his friend's thoughts immediately but skirted it in his reply. "Yeah," he answered. "She's a hitchhiker, I guess, staying in the old Rogers place because she can't afford something better. She's taking in sewing to raise money. In fact, she's done some for us, and Mom says she does excellent work. I've had a chance to talk to her a bit—she's a very likeable person. Why did Dr. Liskowski happen to mention her to you?"

Tom turned his head to study the dawn sky intently. "Well, you know, she just thought it was kinda odd, somebody showin' up just now who's from Transylvania, with all the kinds of things they say about that place in movies and horror stories and with all the stuff that's been goin' on. Fact is, I didn't even know it was a real place, 'til she told me she'd been there herself."

"Did she tell you that Ana is some kind of raving lunatic who goes around biting cats in the neck for their blood, Tom? And do you believe it?" Joshua said bluntly, some sharpness coming into his voice.

"Actually, she said a human bite wouldn't make that deep a puncture," Tom replied in an even tone. "It'd have to be done with somethin' like a nail or an awl. Why would anything she might've said upset you, Josh? Did I say I'd made up my mind to believe her?"

"No, you didn't," Joshua replied, his voice resuming its usual mildness, "and I know you aren't the sort to jump to unfair conclusions. But some people are." He gave Tom a quick account of the conversation at lunch in Cranesville the day before. "I didn't mean to bite your head off," he concluded, "But I hate to see Ana picked on. I mean, I can tell she's had a lot of sorrow in her life. I know she's lost her mom, maybe other family, too, for all I know. She can't help where she comes from, and I'm sure not everybody from there is a psychopath that acts like a vampire, so I don't see why anybody has to dump any more on her. Besides, if you got to know Ana, talked to her a little, like I have, you'd know that she isn't crazy. And that she doesn't have it in her to hurt a dumb animal just for the sake of it, like this kook that killed the cat did." For Joshua, this speech had been a long one. A little breathless—not from any exertion, but from the strength of his feeling—he fell silent.

A slight smile played over Tom's lips as he answered. "You seem to be just a tad taken with her," he said mildly.

Joshua felt a moment of consternation at hearing his feelings bluntly identified, then shrugged. "Well, I suppose maybe I am. But that's not the point. I just don't want anybody blamed for things they didn't do because of some silly coincidence."

Tom nodded agreeably. "Me either, buddy. In a case like this, it's my job to check on anybody and everybody that isn't from around here. But that doesn't mean I'm gonna accuse anybody of anything unless I've got something solid to go on. I'd like to meet this Ana, but she's got nothin' to worry about from me if she's the kind of person you say she is. And I've always thought that you're a pretty good judge of character."

"Yes, I am," Joshua replied with a grin. "I picked you for a best friend, didn't I?"

"Hey, I can't argue with that," Tom said. By now, they had reached the dense growth of brush and small trees that covered the steep banks of a ravine, slanting down to the creek. A narrow footpath led down to the stream itself, which flowed into the Mississippi a few miles to the east. The light of sunrise fell full on the wide, deep water, turning the surface, which had appeared black a few minutes before, into a shimmering mirror of silver and golden light. At the path's end, a widening of the ravine allowed the water to spread out into a pond, overhung by aged weeping willows, their heavily leafed, whip-shaped branches faintly reflected around the rim.

After removing the two bait cans, Joshua bent and filled the pail with creek water. "Now," he declared, seating himself on a rock worn smooth by years of fishermen's bottoms, "I'm ready to catch supper."

"You and me both," Tom answered, slapping him on the back and preparing to move to his accustomed seat further upstream. "But first," he added with a wink, "So I know what to expect when I meet her, tell me something: is this girl Ana pretty or homely?"

In the act of baiting his hook, Joshua looked up and smiled. He knew his friend's question was only banter, but his answering tone came out unexpectedly warm and serious. "I think she's the most beautiful woman I've ever seen in my whole life."

* * * *

Hours later, Joshua was aroused from a half-doze by a jerk on his line and realized that his yellow-and-white floater had disappeared beneath the creek's surface. "I've got another one, Tom," he called. "If I land him, he should just about fill that pail!" As he methodically worked his reel, hard enough to tire the struggling fish but not hard enough to break the line, he heard Tom scrambling across tree roots and grass tussocks to join him. Just as the lawman reached his side, Joshua hauled his dripping catch from the water. The black speck at the end of the first dorsal fin told him instantly that the fish was a perch.

"All right," Tom cried admiringly. "That's a nice one! I'd say he's six inches long if he's an inch."

"I do believe he's the biggest perch I've caught today," Joshua said. Lifting the lid over the pail, he slid the hook from the mouth of the still-living fish and dropped it in, above the foot-long bass Tom had caught a while before. The latter's characteristic speckled scales glinted green in the sunlight as it wiggled slightly.

"These babies'll be good eatin' when Molly gets done fryin' 'em up for supper," Tom said, smacking his lips.

Joshua nodded, glancing at his watch. "This pail won't hold any more, and it'll take a while to clean these. Let's head for home." Rising, he looked over and saw Tom suddenly stand still, sniffing the air.

A slight frown came to the sheriff's face. "You smell somethin' out of place? Kinda like rotten meat or somethin'?"

Joshua sniffed and nodded. "I've been smelling it off and on since the sun got high, depending on the wind, I guess. What do you think it is? Dead animal, maybe?"

"Maybe. Anyway, the wind's blowin' from over that way. And you see that pile of dead leaves and weeds? You ever hear of leaves and weeds pilin' themselves up naturally, without some help?"

Joshua raised his brows, exchanging glances with his friend. "Let's go over and check it out."

Tom led the way to the pile, half obscured in a stand of bullweed and thistle, a few dozen feet away. They began to dig through the dead leaves and already wilted greenery. Within a minute or so, Joshua's questing fingers touched fur, and cold flesh beneath it. His eyes told Tom what he had discovered. In another few moments, he exposed the lifeless carcass of a dog to full view. The animal had been a mongrel, perhaps part hound and part German shepherd by its look. There was no sign of any wound on the body.

"What do you make of it?" Joshua said.

"Well, it's one of those wild dogs folks've been complainin' about. See, it's got no collar." Tom gestured, touching the neck already stiff with rigor mortis. Abruptly, he caught his breath, his fingers quartering minutely over the area they had felt. He parted the fur and motioned to Joshua. "Look at this," he whispered.

Joshua looked, knowing what he'd see. Like tiny red eyes, two puncture marks looked back at him.

Werner Lind

Chapter Eleven

Emerging from her lightless, musty resting place a few minutes after sunset, Ana closed the cellar door behind her and walked into the main room of the ruined house. She picked up the copy of the paper Joshua had left on the previous evening. With this, along with the electric lantern and a shirt she'd finished mending, she walked slowly outside and around the house to the porch, where she seated herself on the steps. Did she look, she wondered, as hag-ridden with worry as she felt? Since the night before, the certainty that Leah Liskowski suspected her secret had preyed on her mind much more than any concerns about Itchy. That lout did not know where to find her, but the woman scholar did.

But for this fear, her circumstances would not have been wholly unpleasant, even in this time and place which would take a while to get used to. Her shelter was as comfortable as could be expected without her coffin, she had a source of needed income, and she had the opportunity to learn to read, while Joshua—but Joshua's attractiveness was of no relevance one way or the other, she reminded herself. Yet these were meager gleams of cheer in her prevailing darkness, alongside the overshadowing fear of what this "parapsychologist" woman might do, or incite others to do.

It would not do to let Joshua suspect this fear, however. The sound of wheels on the road reached her ears before long, as she had expected, and she resolutely suppressed her unease. She was soon aware that the sound was made by two approaching vehicles, not just one. When Joshua's familiar blue conveyance stopped at the road's edge, the second, a green one shaped more like Dr. Liskowski's, pulled up behind it. She recognized the first person to emerge from this vehicle as Joshua's sister. Its driver, who came around to Molly's side with Joshua a moment later, was a young man Ana had never seen before. He was tall, though a bit shorter than Joshua, and broad-shouldered, with dark hair and a moustache. Though the additional visitors were unexpected, their manner did not appear menacing, which allowed Ana to relax slightly. Frowning with curiosity, she called simply, "Good evening to ye all."

"Hi, Ana," Joshua replied, leading the others up the path. "You know Molly, and this guy here is my friend Tom Saddler. Tom's our sheriff."

"Indeed?" Ana said, quirking one eyebrow as her relaxation evaporated.

"Yes. Anyway, he's taking Molly to the drive-in tonight, but he said they had a little time before the movies start, and he's interested in meeting you. So when

I mentioned I was coming out here, he asked if he and Molly could come along—I didn't think you'd mind."

"Oh, nay, I do not," Ana replied quickly, not with entire truthfulness, as she awkwardly returned Molly and Tom's nods of greeting. Manners here, she was realizing, were less formal than what she was used to, and the difference left her unsure of exactly how to act. "I regret that I canst not offer ye chairs, but ye be welcome to sit on the porch step."

"Porch step'll do just fine," Tom Saddler said immediately. "You couldn't ask for a nicer night to sit outside and enjoy the evenin'." Molly seated herself on Ana's left, and Tom took his place on his companion's other side. Ana noted the tender way his hand brushed the young woman's arm for a moment. A courting couple, she sensed. Well, she wished them joy of each other, with an honest heart and no begrudging. Her eyes automatically slid to Joshua, seated on her right. She found him looking at her, and lowered her glance.

"I hear you're from Eastern Europe, Ana—you don't mind if I call you Ana, do you?" the sheriff said. She shook her head, and he continued with apparent casualness. "You've sure come a long way from home."

You know not the half of that, Ana thought, her eyebrow twitching again. "Aye—t'was my thought to travel awhile, and visit lands I had never seen. Your country is most fair to see."

"Uh, yeah, I guess folks like me that grew up around here kind of take it for granted," he answered. "You must've come over on a tourist visa, then?"

Ana stared blankly at her questioner, not sure what manner of vehicle a "tourist visa" might be, but unwilling to ask lest the answer be something she was assumed to know already. "I came over on a ship," she said simply, after a pause.

At this evidently unexpected answer, Tom paused himself. "Er...no, I was talkin' about your papers—you know, the ones they gave you that allowed you to enter the country?"

Natively quick-witted, Ana recovered swiftly. "Ah, yes, those papers, to be sure," she said agreeably. "I did indeed come hither on a...tourist visa, sir sheriff."

He scratched his well-trimmed moustache thoughtfully and regarded her intently in the dimming light. "Just call me Tom, most folks do," he replied. "You must have to keep those papers with you all the time, just in case you'd ever be in a situation where you'd need 'em?"

Ana glued her eyes to the darkening western sky. "Are not yonder clouds a fair sight? In truth, ...Tom, I have not the papers anymore," she answered, improvising as rapidly as she could. "Some days agone, I was robbed upon the highroad, and my purse stolen. They were inside it. 'Tis for that cause that I be in such short straits now," she added, pleased with that sudden inspiration.

"Oh, Ana," Joshua exclaimed, his face and tone reflecting such concern that she instantly felt guilty over her deceit. "That must've been a horrible experience for you!"

"I should say!" Molly echoed, giving Ana's arm a comforting pat. "With all the nuts running around nowadays, you're lucky you were just robbed, and not hurt."

Ana noticed, though neither Joshua nor his sister appeared to, that the sheriff had not yet reacted verbally to her words. She avoided looking at the man, but felt his stare.

"You reported the robbery to the police in the place where it happened, I suppose—uh, whereabouts did it happen, by the way?" he said, his tone expressionless.

"Some fifty or sixty miles to the west of here, but I know not where exactly. 'Twas on a country road that seemed to be but little traveled; I had not been upon it myself, but that I had lost my way in the darkness. Even did my life depend upon it, I misdoubt if I could retrace my steps thither. And nay," she added, "I reported not the matter to anyone. Alone and friendless in a strange land as I was, I knew not whither to go to do so, nor whether I would be believed. And there seemed to be but little use in telling anyone, for 'twas dark when it happened, so I saw not the faces of the highwaymen."

"You're not friendless now, Ana," Joshua said, softly but with earnest conviction. Ana managed to flash him a brief smile before the sheriff spoke again.

"Well, that robbery was a real shame, and it's mighty con...I mean, inconvenient that you didn't get a good look at the guys who did it. I'd kind of hoped that you could come over to the courthouse and look through some of the photographs that I've got of known felons, but I guess there's no point in that. And you didn't get their license number either, I suppose?"

Ana cleared her throat. "No."

"Not to change the subject," Molly put in, "but, Tom, hon, you and I had better get going. I know they won't start the movies 'til it's full dark, but it will be before long." Tom nodded reluctantly.

"What's playing tonight?" Joshua inquired. "Isn't the first feature that thing about the dogs and cat that get lost in the wilderness?"

Tom snorted disgustedly. "It was supposed to be, but they changed it at the last minute to take advantage of all the garbage that's been in the papers and on the radio about vampires and stuff. First they're showin' *Buffy the Vampire Slayer*."

"Ana, are you okay?" Joshua interrupted in sudden alarm.

"Yea, v-verily," she answered, understanding his thought though not his idiom and speaking without—she hoped—noticeable hesitation. "Methought I saw a serpent moving in the grass yonder, but now I see 'twas but the stirring of the breeze." She slid her hands under the paper in her lap to hide their trembling.

"Any snakes you see around here are mostly garter snakes, which aren't poisonous and are pretty much afraid of people," Molly assured her kindly. "We hardly ever see any rattlers. Hon, we've got to get going." She rose, and her companion followed suit, though Ana sensed he would rather have stayed where he was. "It was good to see you again, Ana."

"And I enjoyed meetin' you," Tom said politely. "We'll have to talk again sometime soon; you can tell me more about the robbery."

"Surely," Ana murmured unenthusiastically. "Fare you both well, until we meet again." She hardly heard the couple as they and Joshua took leave of each other. Her attention was more pressingly occupied in trying to master her nerves, and in considering the questions that swirled in her mind. Who was this 'vampire slayer' of whom the sheriff had spoken? How immediate was the threat? The noise of the green vehicle's departure recalled her attention to her surroundings. Joshua exchanged a wave with Tom as the latter turned his machine into the road to round the bend and disappear.

Alone with Joshua, some of Ana's unease abated. Somehow, she felt a subtle kind of security in his presence. He gestured now to the paper in her lap.

"Have you been reading that since I was here last?"

She nodded. "I have read somewhat—it groweth easier with practice, methinks. And I had naught with which to sew, save to finish this." She handed him the newly-mended shirt.

"Thanks, Ana, I'll wear it tomorrow. That reminds me, I've brought you something." From his back pocket, he produced a small paper packet, which proved to contain several small spools of thread, each a different color, and a tiny sewing scissors.

"Thank you, Joshua," Ana exclaimed. "These be the colors I need, in sooth."

"Well, I thought I'd save you a trip, because I didn't like to think of you going into town by yourself," he said seriously. "The general store's right across the street from Callan's Tavern, where Itchy hangs out a lot. And he's likely to be even more off the deep end when word gets around about the dead dog Tom and I found this afternoon over by Clay Creek."

Startled, Ana looked at him intently. "Tell me of what ye found," she urged, knowing full well what they must have found but more concerned with what they had concluded from it.

Simply and directly, Joshua recounted the discovery of the animal's carcass and how they had taken it to the vet, who was apparently a sort of physician for animals. "Nobody really knows what killed the poor animal, any more than anybody knows what killed that cat the other day," he finished. "But this is going to stir people up all the more."

"Both the animals were strays, were not they?" Ana said quietly, voicing a concern that had nagged at her. "They were...well, neither was a child's pet, wast it?"

Joshua shook his head. "They were both strays. In fact, they're probably both better off dead. You've got a kind heart to think of that, though, Ana," he added softly. Abashed, she dropped her glance. When she raised her eyes again, she found him looking at her intently. "Ana, I think...well, I mean, you come across to me as...the kind of person who wouldn't hurt an animal...." His voice trailed off, leaving the unspoken question sensed as surely as if it had been spoken.

As they looked into each other's eyes, the direct lie that had come instantly to Ana's mind died in her throat. After a moment's pause, she swallowed hard and spoke. "As I grew up, Joshua, it fell to me to help my family in butchering sheep and goats, but oftentimes when I did, I had to—how say it you in English?—to cast up my stomach for pity of the poor beast," she said truthfully. "Doth that tell you something you would wish to know?"

He nodded wordlessly, seemed about to speak again but checked himself, and for just an instant touched her hand, very gently, before withdrawing his fingertips with an embarrassed air. He took a small tablet of blank paper from his pocket. "Uh, well," he said quickly, "Shall we have our next reading lesson? Read me what you've read since the first one."

For the next half hour, the two were busily engaged in the tasks of teaching and learning, as Ana read the many sentences or parts of sentences she had deciphered the evening before. With her innate intelligence and knack for learning language, she proved herself an apt pupil.

Finally, Joshua sat back and began to turn the pages of the newspaper, clearly looking for something. Soon, he apparently found it. "You can already sound out short words really well, Ana," he said, "and that means you can sound out long ones, too, because the rules are the same. You're ready to start reading whole paragraphs. Here—read this ad." He passed her the section of the paper he had been searching for.

She followed his pointing finger, studying the words in the lantern light. "Be that a long 'a' or a short?"

"Long. And the 'i' in the next word is long, too, and the 'gh' is silent."

"Ladies' night at Riv-er Val...Valley...er..."

"Long 'o,'" Joshua interjected softly.

"Rol-ler Rink? Tu-es...Tuesday, Ap-ril...I canst not yet read the numbers."

"You'll learn those next. It's this coming Tuesday."

"Ah-l...all ladies...skate?—long 'a' and silent 'e,' yes?—free. Joshua, what meaneth these words?"

"It means that on Tuesday night, ladies can skate for nothing. Only the guys have to pay," was the reply. When she still looked at him blankly, sudden understanding spread over his face. "I get it. You don't have roller skating in your country, do you?"

Ana shook her head. "Nay. Ice skating we have, but of course that be done in winter. What is this 'roller skating' that is spoken of?"

A twinkle came into Joshua's eyes. "It'll be easier for me to show you than to try to describe it. If you're curious, why not come to the roller rink with me Tuesday night and try it firsthand? It'd really be a pleasure to take you there, Ana," he added, in a suddenly earnest tone which made her look away again. "I think you'd have a really good time, and maybe forget some of your troubles for a while." Seeing her hesitate, he adopted a persuasive, half-bantering tone. "Come on, Ana—you're not going to tell me a lady who traveled halfway around the world just to see places she never saw before would pass up a chance to experience something new, when it doesn't even cost a thing?"

The credibility of her supposed reason for coming here, Ana told herself quickly, ought to be maintained. And after all, why should going to this 'roller rink' with Joshua create any more danger of unwise involvement than accepting a reading lesson from him? It was not as if he had invited her to the Maiden's Fair! "Ah—at what time would you wish to set forth?"

"About the same time I came by here yesterday and today, say six-thirty or so. You'll come, then?" he added, beaming.

She nodded. "Yes, be it so. Come you then, and I shall be ready." As soon as she spoke, the pendulum of her thoughts swung again. But the acceptance was already spoken. With those words, she realized amid a tumult of conflicting feelings, she had opened a door, and on the other side waited—what?

Werner Lind

Chapter Twelve

In Meriwether, as in many small Midwestern towns, the Methodists were easily the largest denomination in the community. Zion United Methodist Church's large sanctuary was filled with some 200 people as the song leader, Percy Crown, came to the lectern to announce the closing hymn. Joshua rose with the others. His strong tenor blended with his mother's and sister's rich altos and Tom's deep bass, singing the familiar words by William Cowper:

"There is a fountain filled with blood,
Drawn from Immanuel's veins,
And sinners plunged beneath that flood,
Lose all their guilty stains."

In spite of himself, the reference to blood made Joshua's thoughts wander on the next verses. Vividly, he recalled the strange events of the last few days. Glancing at the bright crimson of the carpet and the padding on the pews, which showed up starkly against the pale white walls and the very dark wood of the fixtures, he was reminded again of blood. He was recalled to the here and now when the music of the organ fell silent.

When Reverend Evan Shipreeve had pronounced the benediction, the church's electrically-operated carillion began to chime and the worshipers began to file out. "I always enjoy Palm Sunday services," Mary Davidson remarked, as she stepped into the aisle ahead of Joshua. "The Sunday school children were so cute when they marched in with the paper palm branches they'd made. I only wish Ana had accepted your invitation to join us, Joshua."

Joshua sighed softly. "So do I, Mom," he said. He'd extended the invitation on the evening before, just before returning home, but Ana had gently but firmly declined, stating simply that she attended only the Orthodox church. Yet he had vaguely sensed that there was some other unspoken reason for her refusal.

"Well, she's old enough to decide for herself what she wants to do," Molly observed from just behind Joshua, where she and Tom were walking arm in arm.

"I know," Mary replied. "But there's no Orthodox church around here, and I feel it's a pity for her to miss worshiping with other people on that account. Martha! How are you?"

Stopping here and there to shake hands and exchange greetings with neighbors and friends, the four gradually made their way into the church's foyer. As they passed a knot of townsfolk in animated conversation beside the empty coat racks, Joshua heard a reference to the bloodless dog, and something about vampire bats. Along with his family, he exchanged the usual courteous handshake with the minister at the ornately carved front door and descended the short flight of steps outside. A cool breeze—a welcome change from the unseasonable warmth of the previous few days—blew against his cheek, whispering a promise of rain. The church's tall spire, pointed upwards like a black-tipped finger, cast a long shadow over the parking lot on the building's west side. Tom walked along with Molly as Joshua dug his keys from his pocket and led the way to the parking spot where the Davidson pickup waited, next to Tom's car.

"Hon, if I didn't have to work after lunch today, I'd ask you to come over this afternoon," Molly said, giving Tom a pat on the arm.

He smiled understandingly. "I know how it is. In some jobs, you just can't work a normal schedule." The abrupt beep of his pager momentarily startled them all. "Speakin' of which...."

The sheriff quickly threw open the driver's door of his vehicle and flipped the switch of the two-way radio, a duplicate of the one in his official car. "Mother Hen, this is Big Rooster." The answering voice of Grace Pettigrew, the sheriff's department dispatcher, crackled from the receiver. It was too low-pitched for Joshua to distinguish the words, but his eyebrows rose at Tom's next question.

"Breakin' in? Where? All right, I'm on my way. Call Walter in case I need backup." He switched off the radio and turned to speak through the open car door. "Grace got a call sayin' somebody's sneakin' around the old Rogers place. From the description, it could be Itchy."

"I'm coming too," Joshua announced firmly. As he'd expected, his mother and sister both began to protest. But somewhat to his surprise, Tom only gave him an appraising glance, then nodded quickly.

"All right; I don't have time to argue about it. Just don't get in the way if there's trouble."

Nodding gratefully, Joshua thrust the truck keys into Molly's hand and ran around to the passenger side of his friend's car, aware that both women were talking at once, but not taking the time to register what they were saying. Pressing down on the gas pedal, the sheriff pulled into the street as soon as Joshua had fastened his seat belt. "This baby doesn't have a siren like the department's cherry-top does," Tom commented, "But for what little traffic there is on a Sunday, we won't need one, anyway."

Joshua nodded. "Who was it that called Grace?"

"She just said it was a woman. Might've been Ana, if she could get to a phone, but more likely it was someone who lives around there." While he was speaking, he swung the car around the corner of Walnut and Main and picked up speed. "You suppose Itchy might be thinkin' of carryin' out some of those things he talked about seein' at the movies?" he said, without taking his eyes off the road.

"I wouldn't put it past him," Joshua replied, his voice sounding as tight as his stomach muscles felt. "What I'd like to know is how he found out where Ana is."

Tom had no answer for this, and neither of them spoke further until the car slid to a stop in front of the deserted structure that had once been a home. As Tom reached under the seat for his holster, Joshua barreled out the passenger's door. Reaching the steps before Tom did, he reluctantly paused to allow his friend to precede him.

The sheriff tried the door handle. "Locked," he said tersely. "Come on around here, where the wall's fallen in. And stay behind me!" Rounding the corner of the house, they swiftly entered the gloomy, dank-smelling interior.

They crossed the front room, which was empty except for the electric lantern and the brown paper bag which Joshua recognized, set forlornly against the wall next to the hearth. As soon as they moved on into a hallway, he became aware of a steady scraping noise. It was coming from a room, the door of which stood open, near the back of the house. With a quick gesture for Joshua to follow, Tom impatiently brushed hanging cobwebs out of his face and slipped to the open doorway. In seconds, Joshua reached his side, and gasped involuntarily.

Across the room, at another door which was shut, Itchy was crouched, trying to pry the door's hinges free from the wall with the claws of a hammer. Alerted by some sound, he straightened and wheeled suddenly to face the newcomers, eyes gleaming with malevolence. One hand held the hammer menacingly, and the other clutched what looked like a croquet stake with its pointed end whittled to an ugly-looking sharpness. His popsicle-stick cross hung on the outside of his T-shirt, which was emblazoned with the name of his favorite rock group, the Brain-Dead Homicidal Rapists, and featured realistic images of mutilated female corpses.

"Uh, mornin', Itchy," Tom said dryly, laying one hand on the handle of his pistol with apparent casualness. "Would you mind tellin' us what you're doin' here?"

"I'm savin' everybody in this county from the blood-suckin' vampire that's hidin' out here, ya tin-badge jerk!" Itchy growled. "And that crazy religious nut standin' next to ya's in cahoots with her—he probably finds victims for her or somethin'."

"What are you talking about, Itchy?" Joshua demanded, with a sudden sinking feeling in the pit of his stomach.

A self-satisfied smirk oozed across Itchy's features as he mechanically reached up and scratched at his head. "I figgered out what was goin' on after ya ran your mouth Friday defendin' this stinkin' monster—I figgered the two of ya was mixed up together. So I followed ya Friday night. Yeah, that's right," he added in belligerent exultation, as a sick look settled on Joshua's face. "I followed ya –and I seen ya talkin' to your big-toothed girlfriend out on the steps there! And I'd 'a been back here Saturday to settle her if I hadn't got drunk and been too hung over to get here. But I'm here now, an' she's had it!"

"Now, do I understand correctly that you're referrin' to Miss—" Tom began, with deceptive mildness.

Itchy looked at him contemptuously. "I'm referrin' to that big, tall black-haired broad that talks funny, that Davidson's been hidin' in this old dump. It's her that's been killin' them animals around here, and she's gotta be behind that door—it's the only one in the place that's locked. She's lyin' in there, waitin' for the sun to go down so's she can come out and kill people! Saddler, ya gotta help me break the door down, so I can pound this stake through her heart."

Walter Andersen's slightly shrill voice sounded abruptly from outside the front door. "Tom! Tom, you in there?"

"It's locked, Walter," Tom called. "Come around the north side."

"Are ya gonna help me or not?" Itchy bellowed, adding, in a more diplomatic tone, "You're a cop, ain'tcha? Man, it's your job to proteck real people like us from monsters like her."

Tom shook his head, his tone unchanged. "Well, now, I just don't know about that, Itchy. I don't recall readin' anything in the Code of Iowa dealin' with vampires." His voice hardened on the next sentence. "But I have read some things about attempted breakin' and enterin' and threatenin' to do grievous bodily harm, and you're under arrest on both charges. So unless you want to add resistin' arrest to that list, you'd best put your toys down and take a ride to the courthouse."

His face slowly reddening with rage, Itchy threw his hammer and croquet stake to the floor, snarling an obscenity.

"Watch your language while you're in my department's custody," Tom said levelly.

"You think you're real cute, don't ya? I got news for ya—it ain't a crime to kill a vampire! They do it all the time in the movies. Just wait'll I tell the judge all about this!"

"Yeah, Itchy, that should be real interestin'. It'll be hard to wait for, but I reckon we'll have to." At that moment, Walter burst into the hallway, his revolver drawn. Tom motioned to him. "Put the piece away, Walter, and take Mr. Bruggenhorst into custody. You got your Miranda card? Good. Then read him his rights, and take him to the office. I'll be along directly to book him."

Itchy shoved Joshua roughly as he passed him, and indignantly jerked loose from Walter's hand as the officer herded him up the hallway. "I ain't crippled, ya fool! And put that card away—I've heard it enough times already. You ain't heard the last of this, Saddler!" Even after the front door closed behind the two men, Itchy's curses were still audible for several moments, fading away only when a car door slammed.

Shaken by the danger Ana had been in, and more so by his own unwitting part in it, Joshua turned to Tom. "Do you still need to do anything here?"

"I need to pick up the hammer and stake, but I'll come back and do that after I get a couple of evidence bags. What I'd like to do now is find Ana, wherever she's got to, and then find out who called in the report and get a statement from her—we'll check at the houses around here...." He broke off as the front door swung open again, revealing the spare figure of Leah Liskowski. As both men started, she made a reassuring gesture.

"Good afternoon! Pardon my not standing on ceremony, but I'm anxious to see if I was able to prevent some sort of tragedy just now." Seeing their puzzled looks, she quickly added, "It was I who phoned your department a few minutes ago, Sheriff."

Chapter Thirteen

Once she had finished vigorously brushing the dirt from the back of her cloak and skirt, Ana once more ascended the uneven, decaying steps of the cellar, moving carefully but sure-footedly in the dark. She realized, with some surprise, that she was looking forward to her reading lesson with Joshua. It was an unfamiliar sensation to wake up looking forward to something.

At the head of the stairs, she unbolted the door, stepped out, and turned to shut it behind her. As she did, one sight swallowed up her whole attention: the fresh, deep scorings gouged into the wood all around the doorknob and keyhole, and around each of the hinges. When she dropped her eyes for an instant, despite the poor light, she could discern, in the dust layer on the floor, footprints besides her own.

How many minutes she stared, dumbstruck, at this mute testimony to mortal danger, Ana did not know. When she could move again, it was to take a step backward, wheel about, and run blindly to the gap in the house's wall and through it into the night. She almost bumped into Joshua as he came around the corner of the house. Her start of surprise at his sudden appearance nearly made her fall.

His face filled with caring and concern, he laid a comforting hand on her trembling arm. "It's all right, Ana. Itchy's in jail. Tom and I waited around to talk to you, but he went back to town to stay at the cells while Walter went to supper. I heard you running just now, while I was sitting outside the door. How'd you get back into the house? I didn't see you go in."

"I...uh, went in the back door. I saw the, the marks upon...one of the doors within, and the prints of feet."

Joshua nodded understandingly. "I'll tell you all about it. Here, you'd best come and sit down while we talk."

Ana let him lead her to a seat on the front step, and listened to his recital of the events that had taken place earlier. "It turned out Dr. Liskowski's been watching this place most of the time, except when she has to eat and sleep, since Friday night. She said she thought the house might be worth observing for a field study of psychic phenomena. Anyway, she parked quite a ways away and was using binoculars; that's why Itchy didn't see her—"

"She was using what?" Ana blurted.

Joshua gestured, putting the circled fingers of both hands to his eyes. "You know—spyglasses. Anyway, she saw what Itchy was carrying and didn't think he was up to any good, so she went to the nearest house and asked to use the phone."

Ana had no more idea of what this 'phone' was then she had of what binoculars might be, but forbore to ask. The gist of Joshua's story was only too clear. An involuntary shudder swept over her frame. "This Itchy be in jail, you say?" she forced herself to ask calmly. "And how long wilt they keep him there?"

Joshua looked down at the still-muddy path in front of him with a frown. It had rained that afternoon, Ana realized irrelevantly. "Probably not very long, I'm afraid. Tom says neither the county attorney nor Judge Holtzmann will take these charges very seriously, because there wasn't any serious physical damage done. He says they'll probably not do anything more than make Itchy swear a peace bond not to bother you; but still, that's a lot better than nothing. Oh, and Tom wants you to come to court tomorrow for the hearing. He was going to ask you himself."

Ana clenched her hands together to hide their trembling, and shook her head decisively. "Nay," she said firmly. "I was not here, and I saw naught. I cannot add aught to what you and Tom shall say. In sooth, Joshua, I couldst not bear to stand up before all the strangers in a foreign court, where I know not the ways, for all eyes to look at me and mark for fault all mine errors of speech and deed. Even in my own homeland, I was never one who liked overmuch to speak before a great throng of folk. Please, ask it not of me, Joshua, I beg thee." She met his troubled eyes with her own distressed ones, and saw his sympathy there.

"Well, then, I won't...but Tom will, when he gets back. Ana, you can't know how sorry I am that I led

Itchy to you. I never dreamed he'd follow me. But I guarantee you, I won't let him hurt you, I promise you...."

Touched by his distress, Ana laid a comforting hand on his arm, as he had done for her minutes ago. They fell silent, and a memory rose....

* * * *

Goat's blood felt warm in Ana's belly, and tingled where it coursed through her thirsty veins as she crossed the shadowed courtyard of Castle Trina. Since the fatal night on which her path had crossed that of Miklos Trina, three months had passed. Winter had been succeeded by the short-lived Transylvanian spring, following a long cold season, and soon to be followed by the burning heat of summer. In the diffuse, silver moonlight, something yellow on the ground caught her eye. It proved to be a dandelion, invariably the first harbinger of the season. With a gentle finger, she softly touched the little plant's golden head. These hardy little flowers had always been Ana's favorite ones, before.... Remembering, she suddenly felt moisture in her eyes. She straightened, scanning the position of the stars. It would soon be morning. It was time to return to the pauper's coffin her frozen, unidentified body had been buried in after the watchmen had found her in drifted snow a few alleys down from the inn. Miklos' servant Janos had dug up that coffin on the very next night and brought it to this place, for Miklos had indeed made her his 'bride', *though 'slave' and 'plaything'*, she thought bitterly, *would have been truer terms.*

Striding up the crumbling steps that led to the ponderous double doors of the castle keep, she seized the verdigrised knocker ring and pounded firmly. She was answered by shuffling footsteps, followed by the scraping of the huge wooden bar on the other side of the door. One massive portal yawned open. Janos, a stooped, anemic old man with white hair and beard and haunted eyes, greeted her with a bow made awkward by arthritis. Not one of the Undead, but a living mortal—for Miklos had never drunk enough of his blood to kill him, only enough to enslave his will—Janos had been Miklos' slave for at least 50 years. Cowering, weak from hunger—since Miklos fed him just enough to keep him from the sickbed—hopelessly eccentric, his human associations practically forgotten, he was a shadow of a man. His one ambition was to escape Miklos' notice as much as possible. Ana felt sorrier for him even than for herself.

"Good morrow, Janos," she said quietly. "Art any of the others returned yet?" As Ana had learned quickly after arriving, the castle housed four other brides besides herself; Miklos' 'honorable' intentions had never included monogamy. The old man shook his head. "Here be something for you," Ana added. From her pocket, she drew a torn hunk of brown bread. "'Twas on the garbage pile of a farm nearabout. The bottom of the loaf had burnt in the baking, but I did bring for you the top."

Janos seized the morsel and bolted it just as a dog would have. "Th-th-thank you, l-lady," he said in his quavering stammer, giving her one of his rare, timid smiles. He moved to shut the door, when Ana suddenly held up her hand for silence. She thought, but was not sure, that from the deep woods beyond the castle's main gate she had heard a faint sound that rose and fell as the wind did, yet was not wind.

"Hear you something, Janos?" she whispered. He cupped his hand to his ear and listened intently for a moment, then shook his head. Janos' aged ears, Ana knew, heard but poorly. But perhaps it was nothing, after all. She glanced across the torch-lit foyer to the hourglass on its stand. "'Twill be dawn soon," she said. "The others will return forthwith; the doors you may as well leave unbarred." Janos nodded.

Crossing the threshold which Miklos' past invitation had made free to her, she entered the great hall, a lengthy, dim expanse where a few wall torches faintly illuminated a fireplace the width of two hay wagons, and a long trestle table dusty with disuse. From one far corner, a door and winding stair led down into the crypt. Halfway across the room, she jumped suddenly, startled by the boom of a gunshot.

As she turned, Janos stumbled towards her side as fast as he could hobble, eyes distended with shock and fear, holding his hands out to her as if for protection. Ana ran back to meet him, then half pulled him along at her side to the narrow, glazed window beside the main doors. Now sounds reached her ears, the noises of running feet and hoofbeats, with cries of "Slay the monsters!" and similar exhortations. One glance outside showed her enough. Miklos Trina, not far inside the main gate, was running at full tilt for the keep, his cloak billowing in his wake. Close behind him was a motley, screaming mob of peasants, clearly visible by the light of the torches some of them waved. Others carried firearms or sharp farm tools; a few brandished makeshift crosses of staves lashed together or held up carved crucifixes. Dread too deep for words fastened itself on Ana's insides.

Forcing herself to move, she jerked around to face Janos. "I-I...I, the m-ma-master...pro-protect...I m-mu-must," he babbled.

Ana gripped him by the shoulders and looked down into his watering eyes. "Hearken to me, Janos," she snapped. "Go you out the rear gate, quickly, and hide you in the woods 'til sundown. I order you! Go now!" Without waiting for his reaction, she wheeled and raced for the crypt door, moving faster than she had ever imagined she could. She half-ran, half-leapt down the winding stairs, and threw open the narrow door at their foot. As she entered the vaulted burial chamber hewn into the bedrock on which the castle was built, distant footsteps sounded above her.

Six coffins lay silently here, in two rows; one was hers, but it offered no haven now. This would be the first place the mob would come to, and sunrise was at hand. Miklos had once told her of a secret passageway dug long ago to offer escape from invading Turks, leading from the crypt to a brush-hidden exit beneath the castle, somewhere along the trail that wound up the steep cliff face on the north side. With desperate urgency, she seized her own casket and slid it—with her strength it was not heavy, but was very awkward in its bulkiness—to the chamber's north wall. Standing on the lid, she reached up to an empty torch sconce, its base carved in the shape of a wolf's head. A great slab of the stone wall slid open when she pushed on the carved muzzle. To pull the coffin into the blackness on the other side of the newly-opened orifice, and to find and pull the lever on the inner side, was the work of only a few moments. She heard another gunshot, and a body falling at the top of the stairs, as the stone slab slid back into place. Then, abruptly, she felt and heard nothing. Before she could enter her coffin, her consciousness was swallowed by the cataleptic blackness that claimed her whenever the sun rose.

When awareness returned, she found herself lying across the lid of her coffin, her arms spread limply and her neck and back aching from the awkward posture. Swiftly, she rose and put her ear to the hidden door, listening intently for any sound, however faint. There was none. Cautiously, she again touched the lever and slid the secret portal open. The sight that met her eyes in the faint light from the stairwell turned her stomach. She felt bloody vomit rise in her throat.

All the remaining coffins had been smashed to tinder, used as fuel for a great bonfire in the middle of the chamber, the huge pile of black ashes still visible. Miklos' other brides, unable to take refuge in the destroyed caskets, would have died screaming as the sunlight fell on them, their bodies dissolving into nothingness. But Miklos had died before sunrise. The half-charred mass of hacked bones in the ashes could have been anyone's, but she instinctively sensed the ownership of the severed skull hung over a torch sconce in the far wall. A small, round hole showed like a third eye between the two larger ones. Evidently the bullet had been made of silver.

Ana stared for a few long minutes at the scene before her, filled almost to choking with feelings, but not sure she could sort them out and identify them neatly. One thing was sure: she was forever free of Miklos Trina…but not of what he had made of her. And there was no reason to think she ever would be free of that—at least not as long as she could still draw a breath.

Some half-burnt candles lay scattered on the stone floor in one corner; the candelabra had apparently been looted. Taking a deep breath, Ana walked over and picked one up, using her pocket tinderbox to light it. *I will walk through the secret passage*, she thought, *and scan the castle from the outside for signs of life.* If not all the morning's visitors had departed, boldly walking up the crypt stairs might not be a wise action. Holding the candle before her, she entered the passage and began to make her way along it.

After walking some distance, she rounded a bend, giving a quickly muffled cry as she nearly tripped over something. No, it was someone, lying inert in what the candlelight showed as a dark pool. The prone figure rolled partly over, looking up with eyes that seemed to have trouble focusing. "An-Ana?" a voice whispered. Her shocked surprise giving way to concern, Ana recognized Maria, one of Miklos' other brides. A fine-figured, attractive Wallachian, who appeared to be in her late twenties though she had been at Castle Trina for over a century, Maria had been Miklos' favorite consort. The dim light of the candle reflected in cold sparkles from the small fortune in gold rings and bracelets, jeweled necklaces, and silver and diamond tiara and combs he had given her over the years. That same light revealed a random pattern of russet stains splashed outward from two dark holes gaping in the embroidered double apron Maria wore, in Wallachian fashion, in place of skirt and bodice. A moan of agony escaped her lips as she fought for breath.

There had never been any fondness between Ana and Maria, who was as cruel as winter to living mortals and fanatically jealous of all the other brides. Yet now Ana knelt unhesitatingly by her side, and raised Maria's head and shoulders to a position in which she could breathe more easily. "Yea, 'tis I. Do not try to speak, I pray you. I'll help you as I may."

"'Twill not be much, forsooth," Maria whispered hoarsely. "My end be nigh whether I speak or not. Is Miklos...?" She closed her eyes for a moment as if in pain when Ana nodded, then opened them again. "I'll be w-with him anon, wherever he be." Her glazed eyes took on a faraway look. "As...I wended home, up the trail without, I came...came face-to-face with one of those thrice-cursed dogs, those...." She choked on blood for a moment, frantically clutching Ana's arm until she could speak again. "He had a...double-barreled pistol...shot me...ere I couldst get hold of him. Bullets...were silver. He g-grinned when he shot me. Wh-When I had fallen, he...did turn me over with his foot...spat upon my f-face. There was...shouting...he ran away hence up the p-path. I d-dragged myself hither. Methinks my b-bleeding ceased whilst the sun was up."

During Maria's rasping monologue, Ana had been unsuccessfully trying to stanch the bleeding with her own handkerchief. But she knew it was not the real problem—the blood oozing from the wounds was not originally Maria's own, anyway. The true problem was the slow poisoning of Maria's system by the silver, and the internal bleeding into the lungs which was gradually drowning her. "'Tis true I can do naught," she exclaimed helplessly.

Maria's fingers clutched weakly at Ana's. "Nay, but y-your being here doth help. I want not to die alone. Oh, Ana, I do hurt so greatly...and I fear so much."

Ana took the limp hand in hers. "I'll not leave thee," she said simply.

Maria tried to answer, then choked on blood again. "I-I treated thee foully...since thee came hither, Ana," she gasped when she could speak again. "I was wrong...forgive me."

Ana looked down into Maria's dark eyes, feeling moisture in her own. "I do, Maria," she whispered softly.

Maria managed a weak smile, then leaned wearily against Ana's breast, exhaling with a bubbling sound as one hand dropped inertly to the stone floor. The next breath did not come, and in the next instant the decay of long years, held in abeyance until now, did its work. Flesh, hair, clothing and shoes that had been Maria's ceased to be in an eyeblink, leaving only undecaying bones and jewelry in Ana's lap or strewn over the dusty rock floor.

For a moment, Ana stared at the still remains, too shocked to move. *That could have been me,* she thought.

Someday it may be me. She wanted to say a prayer, or even make the sign of the cross, over the departed, but could not force her lips or her hands to do either. At the sudden sound of footsteps in the passage ahead of her, she sprang to her feet, then relaxed as she realized that the shuffling gait could only be Janos'. The light of his torch was already visible. His bent, hobbling figure soon came into view. Taking in the scene before him, he approached her silently, then awkwardly knelt before her and kissed the toe of her shoe just as, Ana realized with some shock, he used to do to the toe of Miklos' boots. "L-Lady," he stammered.

Ana bent down, stuck her candle to the floor, and raised him to his feet, firmly but not roughly. "The others art dead, Janos," she said. "Be the villagers gone?" When he nodded, she stroked her chin for a moment, thinking. "Methinks they will not have left Miklos' stallion here," she said finally, "But doth the stable still stand, and be the wagon still there?" He nodded again. After thinking a moment longer, she squared her shoulders resolutely. "Hand me your kerchief, prithee."

Once he had silently complied, she knelt down once more and began to gather the jewelry that glittered on the floor. "Forgive me, Maria," she whispered. What she was doing felt like stealing, but she was desperate, and, she reflected, even if these ornaments remained strewn in this dark passageway forever, Maria could never exult in their beauty again.

When all the jewels were bound up in the cloth, she rose and held it out to the old man. "You art a free man now, Janos, and not Miklos' slave—nor mine. But if you would do me a last kind deed, take this unto the moneylender in the village when 'tis full dark, exchange it for money, and buy a donkey. And look you, use some of what be left to buy a meal for yourself. When you return, we shall hitch the donkey to the wagon, and place my coffin upon it. I'll get into it, and do you cover it with the tarp. Then drive me hence to a seaport, find a ship going to any foreign land, and pay the captain to take the coffin thither. Tell him a countrywoman of yours named Ana Vasilifata will claim it after they have landed. The rest of the money be yours to keep. Wilt thou do this for me?"

Janos' brow furrowed. "B-but why m-must you g-go hence?' he said. "Who-whom shall I s-serve? I...." His voice trailed away.

Understanding, Ana laid a compassionate hand on his shoulder. "If I bide here," she said, "Soon or late will I be hunted down and slain. There be naught for me here." She pondered a moment. "When you have seen me safe on a ship," she said, with sudden inspiration, "Go you to St. Basil's Abbey. Tell the monks you will serve them in the kitchen and garden if so be that they will look after you. They will do that, methinks. Wouldst like that?"

Janos considered a moment, then nodded and smiled faintly. He reached out for the bundle and thrust it into his ragged shirt.

As he turned, Ana stopped him. "Pray you, Janos, do me but one more favor," she said. "Take Maria's bones, and lay them within the crypt—make two or three trips if you must. She would wish that her bones should lie in the same place as Miklos' do, I be certain, but...I want not to go back in thither. And Janos—wilt please say a prayer for her soul, and for the souls of the others? I'll await you here."

"Yea, I-I...I'll do whatsoever I c-can for-for you, l-l-lady." Bending, he gathered up Maria's skull and an armload of bones with his free hand and set off up the passage, his stooped figure disappearing around the turn.

* * * *

The sudden, distant barking of a dog brought Ana's thoughts abruptly back to the present. Joshua, she realized, was still sitting beside her, his eyes saying clearly that he understood the turmoil inside her, and wasn't uncomfortable in sharing a time of silence. Grateful, she managed to give him a slight smile, and slid her seat a little closer to his.

So much had happened since that conversation with Janos, starting with the journey that took her to the docks at Varna, and then the long voyage on the English trading ship. He never knew it, but the ship's captain had good cause to thank her. By the time the lookout had sighted the white cliffs off Dover, she doubted if there had been a single rodent left in the hold. Their blood had been meager fare, but better than going hungry...and far better than doing to anyone else what had been done to her. But England had proven to be no place of safety for her either, she reflected, unconsciously touching the spot on her bosom where the stake had gone in. And would this time and place prove any safer? After the events Joshua had described, she doubted it.

Chapter Fourteen

Normally, Joshua would have walked the few blocks from the Davidson home to the Lewis County courthouse on Main Street. But on this Monday morning, he intended to leave for Cranesville the minute Itchy's hearing was over, so he'd brought his truck. As he drove, he found himself wishing he could see Ana in the courtroom. That, however, would not happen; she had refused Tom's request as adamantly as she had refused his own. For someone as shy as Ana, Joshua thought, testifying at a public hearing would be as severe an ordeal as a flogging. That fact deserved sympathetic understanding, though he wasn't sure Tom fully realized this.

Pulling into the courthouse parking lot, he was startled by the unusual number of cars already there. When he crossed the lot to the courthouse's back door and stepped inside, he found the hallway thronged with people, gathered in clusters around the pop machine and the few benches along the walls, most of them talking excitedly. Some were the usual courthouse hangers-on, retired old men with no other place to spend time. But most were people who seldom frequented the place: high school kids released from classes because of Easter vacation, unemployed bar room and pool hall regulars, housewives towing children and carrying babies.

On his way down the hall to the sheriff's department, Joshua heard snatches of talk. "...says she's a real—" "Aw, come off it, man, there ain't no...." "Well, I don't know about you, but I wouldn't miss...."

By the time he pushed open the door of the low-ceilinged, shabbily-furnished sheriff's office, Joshua realized that he probably looked as dismayed and disgusted as he felt. "Tom," he exclaimed, "All those people out there, are they here for this hearing?"

From behind his cluttered desk, Tom nodded ruefully. "'Mornin', Josh. Looks that way. You know Itchy got one phone call. Well, he made it to that National Tattler reporter out at the motel, and it appears that the reporter got pretty talkative at Callan's last night. That set the grapevine to hummin'. And of course some folks on the staff didn't exactly keep quiet." This last observation was accompanied by a stern glance at Grace Pettigrew, a slender, fortyish woman seated at the radio table across the room. She blushed, and buried her nose in the paperback romance she was reading. "All right, Walter, it's time. Bring the prisoner out here."

"Right, Chief," the deputy nodded, rising from behind his desk.

Tom turned back to Joshua. "'Course, it won't make any difference in the hearing no matter how many people show up to watch it. And I don't think most folks exactly believe all this talk. But it stirs things up, and folks that get stirred up sometimes get out of hand, and you can't always tell where it might lead to. I don't know. Well, that doctor lady said she'd meet us in the courtroom."

The cell-block door opened to admit Walter and Itchy. "Come on, Walter. We'll take the prisoner up between us." Itchy shot his captors a venomous glance, and made an obscene gesture as soon as he saw Joshua.

The young carpenter followed the two lawmen to the office door, their prisoner firmly in tow. When Tom opened the door, Joshua winced at the sudden brilliance of flashing cameras. He recognized "Dusty" Rhodes, Frank Rhodes' younger son and the principal reporter for the Herald, but several other men and women holding cameras or notepads were total strangers until he recognized one as an occasional reporter on the local television news out of Davenport. Somebody standing on the stairs was pointing a camcorder at the door. One man wearing a particularly garish fedora and sports jacket, pushier than the rest, shoved through the crowd to Tom's elbow.

"Sheriff! Sheriff!" he said shrilly above the noisy babble around them, his prominent Adam's apple bobbing like a yo-yo. "Leo P. Waxman, National Tattler. Do you have a statement for the press?"

"I can't imagine why I would," Tom answered dryly, not slackening his stride.

Itchy immediately piped up, though not able to stand still, with the two officers pulling him along. "Why don't ya ask me, huh? I got a statement for your press, and for the whole stinkin' world! There's a real live blood-suckin' vampire runnin' around loose here killin' cats 'n dogs, an' they put me in jail just for tryin' to get her before she gets us! They oughtta pin a medal on me!" Mingled jeers, laughter, and encouraging yells raised a cacophony which almost drowned him out as Tom and Walter began dragging him up the stairs, but he continued to bellow. "You'll see. You just wait—it might be you she bites next, or one of your kids! Folks oughtta thank me! Go over to the old Rogers place and find her! Drag her out 'n kill 'er—"

"Itchy, shut up!" Tom roared, stopping abruptly and jerking the rabble-rouser around to face him. "What you're doin' here is called incitin' mob violence, and if you don't hush it up, I'll charge you with that, too, once we're in the courtroom!"

"How do ya know what he's sayin' ain't true?" hollered a hoarse voice from back near the front doors. Other voices, angry or mocking, immediately rose to outshout the speaker.

Dusty Rhodes shouted up at Tom. "Sheriff, can you comment on the progress of your investigation into the recent unexplained animal deaths in the county?"

"No," Tom snapped, flushing. "Court opens at nine o'clock, and I don't plan to be late."

With the buzzing throng at his heels, Joshua followed the officers and their prisoner up to the head of the curving staircase and across the hall into the double doors of the courtroom. Many of the chamber's seats were already full, and the air hummed with whispered conversation. Exchanging a nod of greeting with Dr.

Liskowski, Joshua took one of the front row seats marked "RESERVED FOR WITNESSES." Tom and Walter seated themselves beside him, after depositing Itchy at the appropriate table in the enclosed area.

A lanky, weak-chinned, thirtyish man with an arrogant bearing, whom Joshua recognized as G. Emmett Slye, the county attorney, turned and, rising from the other table, came over to where the newcomers sat. "Well, Saddler, where's this foreign woman you said was threatened? Doesn't she intend to testify?" he demanded.

"Mr. Slye, the lady's shy, and bein' in a strange country and all—" Tom began.

The lawyer cut him off with a curt gesture. "Well, that's a big help. She doesn't even take the alleged threat seriously enough to appear at the hearing! I swear, I don't know why I put up with these trivial charges you bring to waste my time, anyway. I have a lucrative private practice and a used car business to run. Do you really think I've got leisure to prosecute an attempt to break down a door that was apparently locked by a householder in the nineteenth century, in an empty house nobody even claims, and mere threats made to a transient who pays no taxes to this county?"

"Sir," Tom said, voice carefully level, "Would you prefer I'd wait until Mr. Bruggenhorst over there kills the lady?"

"Well, not that I want anyone killed, of course, but it would certainly be an easier and more significant case to prosecute," the other snapped brusquely. "I should think you could see that for yourself."

As he spoke, the door behind the bench opened, and the rotund figure of the county judge emerged from his chambers. He waddled to his padded, throne-like chair while the gangling bailiff rose, stuck his wad of gum under his seat, and intoned, "Hear ye, hear ye, this district court for the state of Iowa and the County of Lewis is now in session, the Honorable Judge David Holtzmann presidin'. All persons havin' business before this court, draw near and ye shall be heard."

Judge Holtzmann banged his gavel. "Court's in session, be seated," he barked. "The clerk will call the only case on the docket."

The court clerk adjusted her glasses. "Preliminary hearing in the case of the State of Iowa vs. Bruggenhorst," she read.

"I see that the defendant is not represented by counsel," the judge said. "Mr. Bruggenhorst, if you are unable to afford counsel, the court will appoint counsel for you."

"I'm gonna act as my own lawyer, judge," Itchy growled. At this announcement, Joshua knit his brows. Surprised mutters broke out behind him.

The judge banged his gavel again. "Mr. Bruggenhorst, it is my duty to advise you that your lack of training and experience makes it unwise—"

"Aw, come off it," Itchy snapped. "Lack of experience? You know I've been in this stinkin' courtroom a dozen times if I've been once—"

"Then stand up when you address the bench, and don't interrupt me anymore, or I'll jail you for contempt! You're charged with attempted breaking and entering, to wit, of a locked door on the old Rogers property, and threatening to do grievous bodily harm to one Ms. Anna, uh, Vlass-ey-fatta. How do you plead?"

"Not guilty," Itchy replied, less belligerently, and standing this time. "Uh, Your Honor."

"Very well. This is a preliminary hearing rather than a trial, so only evidence against you will be considered. You may waive your right to have this evidence considered by a grand jury."

"Yeah, I do that. Uh, what you said."

"Good. Then sit down. Mr. Slye, you may proceed."

The county attorney rose. "The People call Dr. Leah Liskowski to the stand," he said. She came forward and was sworn. Under his questioning, she stated that on the preceding morning she had been parked in a lane some distance from the old Rogers house, had seen Itchy approach the house in a suspicious manner holding a hammer and stake, and had then run to a nearby farmhouse and phoned the authorities. When she finished, the judge spoke.

"Mr. Bruggenhorst, do you wish to cross-examine?"

Itchy scratched his head vigorously, then came forward pugnaciously. "Yeah, I got me some questions to ask," he said. "The more thinkin' I did about this, the more somethin' started addin' up. You're that Jew woman that's supposed to be some kinda expert on vampires, ain't ya?" Again whispered exclamations rose, and again Judge Holtzmann pounded his gavel.

Leah regarded Itchy coldly over her glasses. "I believe I know something about that subject, yes."

"Yeah? Well, would ya mind tellin' everybody why you was sittin' out in the middle of nowhere watchin' that old haunted house in the first place?"

"I was doing some...research, for my own private study."

"Does your 'research' have somethin' to do with showin' that the bi...uh, woman, that's hidin' out in that house is a real live vampire?"

Mr. Slye was on his feet before Leah could answer. "Objection, Your Honor! This is...well, idiotic!"

"Mr. Bruggenhorst," said the judge dryly, "Is it your intention to lay a basis, through this line of questioning, for an insanity plea?"

Itchy shook his head indignantly. "No! I ain't crazy! I'm tryin' to prove what I been tellin' everybody all along—that this broad's a blood-suckin' vampire, and that I didn't do nuthin' wrong when I went after her! Killin' vampires ain't illegal—for cryin' out loud, that's what regular people is supposed to do to 'em—" He was abruptly interrupted by a commotion at the back of the room.

Swinging around in his chair, Joshua recognized the barrel-chested, bearded man carrying a gunny sack who had just burst through the doors as Paul Garrett, a hog farmer whose property lay north of town. A burly man in his early sixties, Garrett's jaw was now set in determination. He continued his stomping tread up into the partitioned area in front of the bench, ignoring the banging of Judge Holtzmann's gavel. The judge's brows were beetling ominously, and his face was slowly turning red with indignation.

"Garrett," he thundered, "Can't you see we're trying to hold a hearing here?"

The farmer, however, stood his ground. "If you're holdin' a hearin that's got somethin' to do with vampires," he proclaimed in booming tones, "Then I got somethin' here that has to do with that, and you oughtta see it. I found it in one of my fence rows this mornin'."

"This is highly irregular," the judge began, then stared as the older man lifted a dead raccoon out of the gunny sack, holding the already stiff animal up by its banded tail. "I don't want that animal's blood dripped on this carpet—"

Garrett interrupted him impatiently. "No, you don't understand, Judge! That's just it—it ain't got no blood to drip! Look!" Taking his penknife from his pocket, he slashed a deep gash from one of the lifeless joints to the other. The rich, red blood that should have welled up from the slit veins of even a dead animal was noticeably absent. "It's got two holes in its neck, too, like I heard the dead cat and dog had," the farmer added, holding the animal up higher and parting the neck fur.

Shaking his head, Joshua slumped forward dejectedly in his seat, a nauseated, sinking feeling in his stomach which had nothing to do with queasiness in the presence of an animal carcass. He was only marginally aware of the pandemonium of voices, the thunderous banging of the judge's gavel, and the photographers' headlong rush to snap pictures of the grisly object in Garrett's hand. About all his mind could take in at the moment was one desperate question: when—and how—was all this going to end?

Werner Lind

Chapter Fifteen

"Good eve, Joshua," Ana said warmly, as the young man walked up the path to the old house's porch at the hour at which she had come to expect him. Though he smiled in greeting, she thought his face seemed drawn and tired. "Come, sit here and rest you. Art weary from your day of hard toil?'

He nodded. "A little. How about you, Ana—how was your day?"

"Rather uneventful, in sooth. Here be the mending I have finished thus far, and the rest will be ready on the morrow when you come to take me to this 'roller rink.'" Putting his key ring away in a front pocket, Joshua bagged the folded articles she handed him in a white bag he took from his back pocket. Ana could not guess what it was made of. It looked as thin as paper, but did not rattle as paper would.

"Both Mom and Molly are real pleased with your sewing. Mom says she thinks she can get you some more work, for some of the ladies in her Sunday school class."

"She is most gracious," Ana replied sincerely. Her eyes met his, and held them. "How fared matters this day in the court?"

Joshua cleared his throat uncomfortably. "About as well as could be expected, I guess." Quickly, he ran through an account of the morning's events. "The upshot of it," he finished, "was that the judge made Itchy put up a five-hundred-dollar peace bond, which his dad actually put up for him, that will be forfeited if he bothers you again as long as you're in the county. Itchy still lives at home. If his dad loses money because of this, Itchy's home life isn't going to be pleasant. So I'm hoping that you don't have to worry any more about him. He did make quite a stir with his vampire talk, though. And that dead raccoon didn't do anything towards calming folks down, especially after the other two dead animals that turned up last week." As he spoke, Ana plucked a blade of grass and twisted it nervously around her finger.

"So. The townsfolk hereabout," she said bluntly, though her voice trembled slightly, "Think they that I be...one of the Undead?"

He paused, frowning thoughtfully. "No, I don't believe there are many who really think that," he said finally. "Only Itchy, and maybe a few others. Bottom line, most everybody knows that there can't be any such things as vampires, because...well, because there just can't be. But these animal deaths around here have been strange. And happening like they did just after that armored car accident...well, you know, it makes people jumpy, makes them not know exactly what to believe. I just hope Tom gets to the bottom of this business soon, and puts a stop to it once and for all. It's like living in the twilight zone."

"Aye, well...mayhap the strange deaths of beasts hereabouts will cease, and talk of the matter fade away in due season," Ana suggested, wishing this were actually a possibility. "Now, I would fain ask a favor of you, Joshua." She had finally worked her courage up to this idea—if Joshua and others regularly rode in these horseless carriages, the things couldn't be as dangerous as they seemed. "Later, when you be ready to set out homewards, might I go into the town with you, and couldst set me down at this 'general store' you spoke of? Needs must I buy some soap, and a comb as well. 'Twill be no trouble for me to walk back hither, but 'twould save me time and steps if I may go thither in your...vehicle." Even before he answered, Joshua's smile made it clear that he was pleased by her request.

"Sure, I'll be glad to take you into town. And things being like they are, you're better off having, well, having somebody with you when you go, in case you do run into Itchy. But you're not going to walk back here, either. I'll be more than glad to bring you back. We'll just quit our reading lesson a little early. Speaking of that, have you been reading any more in the paper?"

* * * *

So it was that Ana, a couple of hours later, found herself a passenger in Joshua's strange conveyance as it approached the edge of Meriwether. Surprisingly, the ride had been quite comfortable, except for her uneasiness at the vehicle's enormous speed. There was much less jolting than there would have been in a horse-drawn wagon. Its enclosed part had windows, much like those of a carriage, with a large one all across the front. She had quickly noted that a mirror hung at the top of this, on some sort of short peg or stem, but this mirror was small and faced the middle of the seat, so that it was not hard to avoid facing into it. The rapidly-changing view the windows presented was rather exciting, though Ana had seen it before on foot and wing. With the moon now full, the wide cornfields, quiet pastures, and heavily overgrown fencerows showed to advantage in its soft light. As they neared the town, the lights along the streets cast a stronger illumination over the scene, in which buildings and signs stood out clearly. One of the latter, which bore the likeness of a large furry animal with an enormous rack of antlers, caught Ana's eye.

"What manner of beast is that?"

"Where? Oh, you mean the sign. That's a moose."

"I see." The sign had carried the words "PROTECT OUR CHILDREN." *A beast with such formidable antlers*, Ana reflected, *could well be a danger to small children—perhaps even to adults*. She resolved to keep an alert watch for it.

"That big building on our left is the consolidated school, where I went all twelve grades," Joshua said. "And the smaller building across from it is the county hospital, where Molly works. She's an LPN."

"She is a what?"

"A nurse. Well, a practical nurse. She doesn't have enough training to be a registered nurse." Ana turned her glance to the side window, partly to keep from missing any of the strange sights, partly to hide her surprise. She had never heard of a female nurse. But she had to admit that it would be more appropriate for women to nurse other women than for men to do so. Perhaps Molly's choice of a male occupation influenced her choice of male attire.

"Your mother spoke of other children not at home, Joshua," she said. "How many other brothers and sisters have you, and live they hereabouts?"

"I've got four brothers, and another sister," was the reply, "but none of them live very close. My brother Jim's in his first year teaching school in Maine, one brother's in the Army and another in the Peace Corps, both overseas, and my youngest brother's in college in Des Moines—Drake University. And my other sister's married and lives in Wisconsin; that's where her husband's from. It's odd when you think about it—I'm the oldest and Molly's next, but we're the ones still in the nest. How about you—do you have any brothers or sisters?"

"I...grew up with ten sisters and seven brothers; I was the youngest. What building is that, with the great red thing before it?"

"That's our volunteer fire station, and that's the engine. When I was a kid, I used to be fascinated with that engine. Even then, I thought about someday being a firefighter. Of course, I pictured it as more exciting than it really is. The general store's in the next block, across the street, that big red brick building."

Following his gaze, she took in the large structure, as big as any two or three of the nearby buildings. Situated on the corner, it bore a painted inscription on the long side facing them. Ana deciphered the words, "JONES BROTHERS' GENERAL STORE. ESTABLISHED 1886." She had barely done so when Joshua brought them to a stop at the curb. While she fumbled with the "seat belt' he'd shown her how to fasten, he went around to the door on her side, then opened it and helped her dismount from the high seat as attentively, Ana thought, as if she were Voivodin of Transylvania.

Smiling her thanks, she crossed the pavement beside him to the building's nearest entrance, where she drew back a little to let him precede her. He pulled open the heavy wooden door, its upper half glazed to make a kind of window. "Come on in, Ana."

Thus invited, she stepped lightly over the threshold, and looked keenly about her. The store's interior was bathed in the same sort of strange light as the streets outside, but more brilliantly; it was also surprisingly cool. No doubt, Ana guessed, both features resulted from some application of the natural magic in which people of this time were so skilled. Floor-to-ceiling shelves lined the walls and were ranged at short intervals across the room, except where a waist-high counter ran to her left. Every available inch of the shelves was crammed with colorful merchandise, recognizable and unrecognizable. Open barrels and boxes stood wherever space allowed, and a faintly spicy smell teased Ana's nostrils. Above her head, the tinkling bell that had sounded when Joshua opened the door fell silent as he closed it behind him.

"Let's see—you wanted soap, and a comb? The soap's over this way." He led the way to the aisle formed by two rows of shelves halfway down the building's front, exchanging nods and greetings with the few shoppers they passed. Ana avoided eye contact with these folk, but could feel their curious stares as surely as if the glances were touches. On the shelf to her right, Joshua pointed out what were apparently fist-sized hunks of soap, completely wrapped in paper. "They've got quite a few brands to pick from."

Ana studied the writing on the wrapping paper of the soap chunk closest to her eye level. "Spell you soap, s-o-a-p? Had I sought to spell it, I should have written s-o-p-e."

Joshua grinned. "That would fit the rule better, wouldn't it? It's what they call irregular—" Ana jumped abruptly, startled by a sudden sound, not particularly loud but unexpected and unlike anything she could describe. He hastened to reassure her. "That's just my pager. Botheration, though—it means there's a fire somewhere. Excuse me just a minute. Ralph, I've got to use your phone." This last utterance was delivered in a raised voice as he hurried around the front corner of the aisle. While she stood uncertainly where she was, she heard his swift footfalls approaching the counter area and, after a few moments, returning. His face, when it came into view again, was troubled.

"Ana, I'm sorry, I've got to go right away. There's a fire over at the trailer park, and people are still in the trailer that's burning. I don't know how long I'll be, but wait here. I'll still take you back—" As he spoke, two thoughts crossed Ana's mind: that the fire would likely take much time to put out and that Joshua would need rest when it was over, and that in the meantime, waiting here to be stared at by shopping townsfolk was not an experience she would relish.

"Nay," she interrupted firmly. "Trouble you not about me. I shall walk back to the old house, and be none the worse for it. Thank you for what you did do. Go now," she added, as he opened his mouth to argue, "lest someone perish whilst you talk! All will be well with me!"

"Okay, okay. I'll see you tomorrow evening!" He turned and hurried away. A minute later Ana, still facing in the direction he had gone, watched him through the huge window as he leapt into his vehicle and roared off in it, quickly vanishing around the corner.

With a sigh, she turned back to the shelves, telling herself that she had made the right decision. Quickly, she selected a chunk of soap, and set off in search of a comb. She found a box of these two aisles over, after passing a display of what looked like imitation eggs in wicker baskets, arranged beneath the effigy of a rabbit whose almost human grin looked quite unreal. Picking up the first comb she touched—they were all identical, small and black—she made her way to the front counter, passing pairs and small groups of people who whispered softly to each other as she went by. The storekeeper, a fat man perhaps in his late sixties, eyed her up and down as she approached and set her purchases on the counter in front of him.

"Will that be all for you, ma'am?" he wheezed. She nodded, and silently offered him the piece of green and grey paper Mary Davidson had given her. Having taken it, he turned to a metal apparatus, and pushed some buttons on the front of it which looked like flat metal mushrooms on short stalks. He placed the paper in a drawer at the bottom of the device, which slid open with a ringing noise, and handed her a few similar papers, along with some dull, counterfeit-looking coins. "You rent that get-up at one of them costume places?" he inquired as she pocketed her change. The vocabulary of the question made no sense to her.

"I crave your pardon, sir?" she said, glancing at him quizzically.

"Oh...never mind," he replied quickly. "Uh, paper or plastic bag for these things?"

"It matters naught." The bag she received was of the same material as the one Joshua used for his mother's mending. She felt it curiously between two fingers. "Plastic," she repeated softly to herself, then looked up and cleared her throat as she felt the man's eyes on her. "Good morrow to you."

"Uh, yeah; the same to you."

As she went out the door, its bell tinkled quietly above her. She turned to face the direction from which she and Joshua had come earlier, and froze in her tracks.

A yard or so from her, three young men, all of them looking slightly drunk, were walking toward the door. One was big and paunchy, with a heavy-browed, stupid face; the second was also of ample build, his buck teeth large and prominent and his expression sour. Ana did not recognize either man, but she easily recognized the third—Itchy. "Bull," he was saying, "you'n Jigger go on to Callan's an' get us sommore booze. I wanna see if

Jonesey's got any more garlic." Turning his head to the
door, he saw her.

Inwardly berating the surprise which had frozen her
for a moment, Ana tried to sidle past him, but he moved
to block her. "You stand in my way, sirrah," she said.
"Prithee, let me pass."

"Uh...say what?" the buck-toothed one mumbled,
blinking.

Itchy grinned ominously, showing yellow teeth.
When he answered, his tone was thick with menace. "Let
you pass? Oh, no, baby. Not hardly. I got me a different
idea. See, I got me somethin' here to handle the likes of
you, ya slimy, blood-suckin'—" Ana did not hear the
obscene epithet he added, for as he spoke he had thrust a
hand into the neck of his filthy shirt, and her whole
attention was fixed on the object he pulled into view. Her
whole conscious mind was seized by the same strangling,
all-consuming terror she had known in the dark crypt of
the chantry. Gagging as she tried to breathe, she gave
ground, half stumbling backwards, then wheeled and ran
headlong, barely seeing or caring where she was going.

The sound of Itchy's heavy footfalls pursued her,
punctuated by a drunken shout from one of his
companions. "Aw, Itchy, don't run her off! She's good-
lookin'!"

As she fled, Ana became aware of an alley, and
turned into its relative darkness. Itchy's footfalls and
profane threats still followed. Halfway down the alley,
she stumbled and fell. Scrambling to her feet, she heard a
sudden rustling from inside a huge metal receptacle a few
feet away, which judging by smell held garbage. Her

drowning mind frantically grabbed this one lifeline of possible deliverance. Her back pressed against a wall, she closed her eyes and sent a message with her mind to the four-footed cause of that rustling, a silent message willed with the whole force of her being. She could feel sweat trickle on her face and back. A moment later, she smelled the odor of beer and bad breath inches from her nose. When she opened her eyes, she immediately closed them again. Itchy had removed the makeshift cross from his neck, and now held it with both hands up to her face, almost touching her. She could sense the murderous, gloating rage in him.

"Oh, you're gonna pay—you're gonna pay in spades, you are, ya monster! Nobody kicks me in the face and gets away with it, and for sure not a woman— Aaahhhggg!"

At this scream, Ana opened her eyes again. Attached by its teeth to Itchy's right arm, its claws raking his dirty sleeve, was a large, red-eyed rat. Dropping his homemade cross, Itchy, still howling, struck at the animal with his left hand. It promptly locked its teeth into that appendage and hung on as he frantically tried to shake it off. With blood spurting from his arm and hand, he screeched a curse, ran at the near wall, and slammed his left hand against it, full force. He accomplished only further injury to himself, however, for at the last moment the frenzied creature released his hand and launched itself downward to a new tooth-hold on his leg. Shouting incoherently for help, and dripping blood with every pace, he half-ran, half-stumbled back up the alley, batting ineffectually at the rodent with his good hand. The animal showed no intention of giving up the attack.

As Itchy emerged from the alley, his cries were taken up by his companions. "Hey, call nine-one-one! Some rat's muggin' Itchy!"

Drawing a gasping breath of relief into air-starved lungs, Ana permitted herself a slight smile of satisfaction before turning and running, with light-footed speed, into the darkness.

Chapter Sixteen

"I sure appreciate the lift, Josh," Joe Carder said quietly from where he sat on the passenger's side of Joshua's truck. He held his right hand up awkwardly in the air where it wouldn't touch his lap or the seat. The flesh of the palm and fingers was visibly seared, and looked as painful as it undoubtedly felt.

Joshua answered in a sympathetic tone. "I'm just glad I can help you out, Joe." The older man's hand had been burned in trying to rescue his daughter from the trailer fire that had apparently been started by the toddler's playing with a neglected cigarette lighter. It had been a miracle, Joshua reflected thankfully, that all four of the trailer's residents had gotten out alive, though the toddler had been rushed to the University of Iowa Hospital in Iowa City for some skin grafts. This had taken Lewis County's only ambulance, and since Mrs. Carder was using her family's only car to drive herself and her son to the Davidson house, where Joshua had offered them temporary shelter, he had volunteered to drive Joe to the emergency room at the county hospital.

"We all appreciate you and your mom lettin' us stay at your place, too," Joe went on. "It'll only be for a day or two, 'til we make some arrangements to stay with the wife's folks over across the river." This designation, as both men took for granted, referred to the Mississippi. Joe fell silent a moment or two, staring thoughtfully through the truck's window into the night. "Thing like this makes ya think, y'know? We all coulda got killed back there."

"That's the kind of thing that makes us all realize how important it is to be ready when our time does come," Joshua said gently.

Joe sighed heavily. "Yeah, I hear ya. I guess I'm what my mom's church calls a 'backslider.'" He paused to blow his nose, holding his handkerchief clumsily in his left hand; he'd been crying quietly earlier. "I believe in God, though. And with my littlest one lyin' in the burn unit at Iowa City, you can bet I'm gonna be in church this Sunday."

Joshua eased the truck into the hospital parking lot. "Well, that's the place to be any Sunday. But you know the paramedics said she'd be all right. And all of us at the Zion Church will be praying for her—for all four of you."

"We can use it. Josh." Joe added suddenly, with even more earnestness, "There's a lot I done in my life that I ain't proud of. Most everybody knows that you're a real religious man. No, that's so," he insisted, as Joshua opened his mouth. "If you ask God to forgive me for the things I done, do you think He'll do it?"

Joshua carefully parked the vehicle, then cut off the engine and met the other man's eyes. "No," he said simply. "But He will if you ask Him to. Here, let me get that door for you." He helped Joe down, then led the way to the building and opened the door that led to the emergency room. "Doc O'Riordan's expecting you. When I phoned, they said he was already here taking care of another case. Molly's on emergency room duty tonight. I guess she's having a busy night of it."

Completion of the paperwork at the admitting counter took only a few minutes, and then the clerk on duty pushed a buzzer. In a moment, Molly emerged through the swinging doors of the emergency room itself, pushing a wheelchair. "Hi, there, Mr. Carder, we've been expecting you," she announced cheerfully. "You get to ride in there in style. I know it's silly, but it's regulations. Joshua, you'll never guess who we got done treating a while ago."

"No, but I know you're going to tell me."

"None other than Itchy, big as life and twice as nasty. Seems a rat that was probably rabid jumped on him in an alley and tore him up pretty bad. He claims Ana had something to do with it—do you believe the nerve of that creep? Well, I'll see you later if you're still up." This last was delivered over her shoulder as she pushed the burn victim through the double doors.

Joshua stared after her in surprise, then turned back to the clerk. "Itchy Bruggenhorst was in here?"

"Yes, sir. They worked on him in there for a while, then sent him up to the regular ward."

"Really? Who's the duty nurse up there tonight?"

"Mrs. Rutledge."

"I'm going up to see him. I expect to be back before they finish with Mr. Carder, but if I'm not, tell him I'll be down to drive him home in just a minute or two, okay? Thanks."

Familiar with the layout of the hospital building, Joshua quickly made his way to the nurse's station in the hospital's main section. As he had expected, he found a thirtyish, dark-haired woman seated at the counter behind a nameplate which read, "Cassandra Rutledge, R.N."

"Hello, Josh," she said brightly, looking up from a magazine. "What are you up to tonight?"

"Oh, about six foot, I guess," he replied banteringly. Then he added, seriously, "Actually, Cassie, I came by to see Itchy for a minute or two, if that's possible. Is he allowed to have visitors?"

"Well, his chart doesn't state any restriction," the nurse replied, glancing at the clipboard beside her. "He had serious wounds from animal bites and gashes, but they've gotten him all stitched up and bandaged. Right now, we're just holding him 'til the HDCV vaccine gets here so we can give him the first injection of the series, in case the animal was rabid. And there isn't much doubt of that, the way it ripped into him. He's in room seventeen. But just now, Mr. Mueller's with him."

Joshua frowned, recognizing the name of the hospital administrator. "Why would Mr. Mueller want to talk to him, and at this time of the evening? Doesn't he usually leave at five o'clock?"

Cassie nodded. "Yes, and he did today, too. It was the other way around. Itchy demanded to see him, and wouldn't take no for an answer. He was raving something about needing protection from a vampire. He said he was chasing her, and she made the rat attack him. Said he'd sue if he couldn't talk to the administrator."

Joshua considered this a moment. *So much for my hopes that Itchy wouldn't bother Ana any further,* he thought. "Is it all right if I wait outside the room 'til they're through?" At her nod, he turned and made his way down the white-tiled corridor that led straight back from the reception area. Room 17 was near the end, on Joshua's left. He heard voices floating through the open door while he was still some paces away. At once, he recognized Itchy's bellicose tones.

"I'm tellin' ya, I gotta have protection! Ain't ya been listenin' to one thing I've been tellin ya, ya du...sir? That rat was sicced on me by a vampire, an' she's gonna come back tonight an' finish the job! Ya gotta get me a cross to put around my neck, an' some garlic—I got some at home—"

"Mr. Bruggenhorst," the administrator's frustrated voice interrupted, "In the first place, we have a security guard in the evenings and the doors will all be locked at ten—"

"She can come through the windows," Itchy shouted.

"They're locked, too, from the inside."

"That ain't gonna stop her! Where you been? Vampires can go right through locks!"

"In the second place, there are no such things as vampires, Mr. Bruggenhorst. Anyone with any education knows that."

"Are you sayin' I ain't educated? What ya think put twenty-seven stitches in me tonight if there ain't no such things as vampires?" There was a slight pause, during which Joshua could picture Mr. Mueller's scathing stare. Then the older man's voice resumed, dripping with scorn.

"In common with the paramedics and with everybody who saw the incident, I believe your injuries were caused by nothing any more supernatural than a rabid rat. As a public hospital, we are not permitted to provide religious objects such as crucifixes to our patients. Nor do any of our staff have time to spare from their duties to fetch garlic for you to smear on our windows. I do not at all appreciate being called from my home to tell you this."

Itchy abandoned any attempt at diplomacy in his reply. "Stuff it, ya dumb idiot! I'll sue the pants off ya, and this hospital, too."

"I'm quaking in my shoes. In the meantime, keep your ravings about crosses and garlic and vampires to yourself, and don't disturb me at home anymore—and for that matter, don't disturb me during my office hours, either—or I'll take measures to have you committed! It wouldn't take any psychiatrist more than two minutes to diagnose you as delusional."

His mutton-chop whiskers bobbing in time to the angry workings of his jaw, the administrator burst out of the room, barely noticing Joshua and almost stepping on his foot before continuing down the hall.

As Joshua entered the room, his brows rose at the sight of the many bandages on Itchy's face, hands, and bare arms. Looking up and recognizing his visitor, the patient scowled and spat an obscenity.

"Does it bother you that much to see me?" Joshua said.

"Yeah, it does, ya stinkin' geek!" Itchy raised one hand to scratch at his hair, then desisted with a snarl, apparently remembering that his fingernails were under bandages. "I know you're in cahoots with the bloodsucker. So, whaddaya think you're doin' in here, anyway?"

"I stopped by to tell you I'm sorry about your mishap with the rat, and that I hope you have a quick recovery."

"Yeah, I'll just bet you do!"

"And to ask you to please leave Ana alone. Itchy, this whole vampire business is crazy. You can't believe that they exist in real life just because you saw one in a movie, or that Ana's one because she comes from Eastern Europe. She's no more some kind of demonic monster than you are. All you're doing is getting yourself in more trouble, and making most people laugh at you. Surely you can't believe that she had anything to do with you meeting up with a rabid rat—"

Itchy silenced him with a voiceless snarl, his expression twisted with genuine hate. "I don't need you to try to run my life or butt into my business. But that's what you do, ain't it? Ya butt your dirty, stinkin' nose into my business now just like ya did when we was kids, don't ya? Only now I don't have to take it from ya."

"What are you talking about?"

"When we was in third grade! I was mindin' my own business, just pullin' the legs off some grasshoppers, an' ya hit me an' made me stop. Don't tell me ya don't remember that, ya lyin' creep!"

Suddenly, Joshua recalled the long-forgotten incident. He gazed at Itchy in amazement. "You remembered that?" he said.

"Yeah, I did! I remember a lotta things—everybody in the whole stinkin' world that ever did me dirty! An' someday I'm gonna get even with the lot of ya. You'll see, ya nerd! An' I'm gonna start with your slimy bloodsuckin' bean-pole of a girlfriend—yeah, don't tell me you two don't have some action goin', jerk-boy."

Joshua felt his face flush dangerously. "Itchy," he said, "I don't have to listen to this garbage—"

"Naw, ya don't! Ya can get your lousy keester outta my room! I didn't ask ya to come in here."

Turning on his heel, Joshua walked out of the room and down the hall to the front door by the nurse's station. He went slowly and took deep breaths in an effort to keep his temper. As he approached the glass door, it swung open and, to Joshua's surprise, a grim-faced Tom strode in. "Hey, Tom," he greeted. "Are you here about Itchy's bothering Ana again?" he added, as that thought suddenly struck him.

Tom, however, shook his head. "Nope, Mr. Itchy's in bigger trouble than that this time. I've got a pot-head from the high school named Kay Standish in custody down at the office. This afternoon, a janitor at the pool hall heard her buyin' dope off another gal in the ladies' john, and called Grace."

Joshua frowned. "But what does that have to do with—"

"I was comin' to that. Kay's scared enough to do a lot of talkin'. Seems her usual supplier's our dear friend Itchy. He picks wild pot in places in the bottomlands, and he's been dealin' it for about two years. Kay says he got her hooked, and he charges more'n she can afford. Last Wednesday night, he was puttin' the squeeze on her uptown in an alley, and he said he'd take certain favors instead of money. When she wasn't too keen on that idea, he told her he'd just rape her anyway. Just then, a young woman fittin' Ana's description stepped up and told Itchy he wasn't goin' to rape anybody. Kay didn't stay around to see what happened. But that's why she was afraid to do business with Itchy again, even after she swiped some of her mom's money." Joshua had listened to this narrative with increasing anger, mixing with surprise at the mention of Ana.

"So that's why Itchy's got it in for Ana," he said softly.

"Yeah, I thought that might account for some of his recent attitude," the lawman said. "I'll need to get a statement from her later, but just now, I've got a warrant for Itchy on drug and attempted rape charges. He's goin' to be a guest of the county for a bit longer this time, and his next phone call had better be to a lawyer, not to Leo Earwax or whatever his name is—"

"Cassie! Cassie!" A woman's sudden, shrill cry cut off whatever Tom would have added. Swinging around, Joshua saw Jill Herndon, one of Molly's fellow LPNs. The young woman was running down the corridor toward the nurse's station, her eyes wide and her blond ponytail bouncing from side to side.

Cassie Rutledge came to her feet in a hurry. "What is it? A cardiac arrest?"

Jill shook her head quickly. "No, no! It's the patient in room seventeen—I mean, he's not in room seventeen! The window's wide open, and there's no sign of him."

Chapter Seventeen

If she had a mirror, and could see herself in one if she had, combing her hair would be a much easier job, Ana thought as she stood in front of the sagging porch of the old Rogers house, running the comb she'd purchased through her dark locks. Of course, it was not as if she were grooming herself for the Maiden's Fair again, nor anything like it. But still, it would not do to be seen in polite company with her hair disheveled, would it? Hopefully, she looked at least respectable. She wished she had another dress besides the one on her back, but at least it was clean. She'd washed it the night before in a nearby creek, using smooth stones and the cake of soap she'd bought, at the same time as she had bathed herself, and then let it dry through the day. Her hand trembled slightly as she plied the comb. Why was she so wretchedly nervous?

Her conversation with the sheriff last night, she told herself as she scanned her dress front for lint. That must be the cause; it would have made anyone nervous. She rubbed her slender fingers over her chin, thinking. He hadn't questioned her account of the incident Kay had described. And, indeed, Ana's account had been truthful, omitting only any mention of Itchy's knife, since she did not want to raise questions as to how she could have broken it barehanded. Nor had he questioned her hesitation in coming forward, once he learned that she had not known what "pot' referred to. For that matter, she wasn't sure she knew now, as Tom's explanation had made little sense. But she was not convinced he believed she had happened to be in the alley only while walking to enjoy the stars. And his insistence that she appear in court to testify against Itchy once that varlet was found was highly troubling. Obviously, she would need to be out of the area before that trial, and such a hasty, forced journey would be fraught with danger. And until Itchy was found, what might he be likely to do? True, Leah Liskowski kept a near-continuous watch on the old house, but that was not an entirely unmixed comfort.

As Joshua's vehicle came into view, Ana pocketed the comb, took a deep breath and squared her shoulders. She walked out to the road's edge to meet him. At the sight of her, his face lit up like a hearth fire fanned by a sudden breath of wind. Halting his traveling machine, he came around to open the other door for her. His tall, strong figure was clad in a shirt and pants that looked to be of finer material than his usual clothing, and he had a freshly-scrubbed look.

"Good evening, Joshua," she said. "You look most comely." Only after blurting this comment did she reflect that it was rather personal, and she felt the usual pallor of her face lessen slightly. But Joshua only beamed with pleasure, and gestured self-deprecatingly.

"Oh, go on. You're the one who looks good, Ana."

The intensity of her pleasure at this compliment surprised her, and she dropped her eyes. "I but wear the only dress I own, and I misdoubt whether mine hair be well-combed even now."

"I think your hair could blow every which ways in a high wind and still look pretty," he answered, then dropped his own gaze and cleared his throat. "Uh, well, are you ready to go?" he added quickly in a brisker tone.

"As ready as ever I shall be, belike," she replied. "How fared the folk where the fire was yestereve?" she said, once they were both strapped into their seats and the self-propelled vehicle was moving back towards the town. "I hope no one was hurt in any wise?"

"A two-year-old girl was burnt pretty badly on the arms and lower body, and her dad had a third-degree burn on one hand, but they say both of them will heal all right," Joshua told her soberly. "The little girl's in the hospital at Iowa City. Her parents and brother are staying with Mom and Molly and I 'til the woman's folks get a place fixed up for them. They say it should be ready by tomorrow evening. The trailer was a total loss," he added, "but luckily they did have some insurance on it."

"I see," Ana replied cautiously, though she didn't. "Hast heard any more news of this knave Itchy?"

Joshua brightened. "Yes—Tom called me earlier, because he thought I might see you before he would. He told you that Itchy evidently stole a car out of the hospital parking lot last night? Well, they found the car today, over in Davenport by a bridge at the river. So Tom figures Itchy crossed over into Illinois on foot and left the car so they couldn't charge him with bringing it across a state line. We don't think he'll be in any hurry to come back. My guess is that you don't have to worry about him anymore, Ana. So I want you to forget him, and just relax and have a good time tonight. You need some enjoyment in life."

"That be sober truth," she agreed softly. "Well, then, Joshua," she added in a brighter tone, "let us do as you say and bid frowns and cares to vanish for a season. You have told me but little of this 'roller skating.'"

"Well, you said you have ice skating in your country? I'd say the two are a lot alike, except in roller skating the skates have little wheels instead of blades, and you skate on a smooth floor instead of on ice."

Ana considered this, then smiled. "Verily, I think it may hold some promise after all."

Joshua looked at her curiously. "I don't know much about your country, Ana. What sorts of things do you do over there for fun, besides ice skating?" Deducing the meaning of the term "fun" from the context, Ana settled back in her seat and let her happier memories arise in her mind.

"When I was a child, we worked much more than we played," she said, "but 'twas not always worktime. My brothers and sisters and I played the sorts of games that children do in every land and ran races, and swam in the stream in summer, and built figures and castles of the snow in winter. On Harvest Day some traveling mummer would bring his tame bears to dance in the streets. And on that day, and on saints' days, all the village folk would dance together—the hora dance, which is very slow and stately, and the invirtita, which is fast and whirling, and many others. At this season, 'twould soon be time to choose the Green George for Saint George's Day." She swallowed hard, willing her eyes not to water. "Come, enough of my memories of childhood, Joshua. Share with me of yours. You grew up here, I know; this place must mean much to you."

"Yes, it does. There's no place I'd rather live, and it's a good place to raise a family in...it was a good place for me to grow up in, is what I mean." Time passed quickly on the drive as he spoke of his father and brothers, of fishing and swimming and tree-climbing, of Christmas caroling and trimming the tree, of 'trick-or-treating' on Halloween, which was evidently another holiday, and of games Ana had never heard of before. 'Softball' and 'football', from his descriptions, sounded enjoyable. She was surprised they had arrived already when he slowed the vehicle to a stop in what proved to be a graveled expanse beside a large, windowless, barn-like building. Its sign bore the same words she had read a few evenings ago, though written in what Joshua called capital letters: "RIVER VALLEY ROLLER RINK."

From inside, strains of music and song reached Ana's ears as she and Joshua approached the doors, which, oddly, were made of solid slabs of glass. As he opened the door, she motioned him to precede her. "You go first," she said shyly.

He smiled encouragingly. "Nobody'll bite you. That's a figure of speech," he added, as she quirked one brow quizzically. As soon as he stepped inside and motioned her to follow, she stepped across the threshold. Immediately, she winced at the chill air inside.

"This air conditioning is kind of overpowering when you first step into it," he whispered. "I think they turn it up too high, but you'll warm up once you get to skating." Ana nodded wordlessly, intent on surveying her surroundings.

They had entered a carpeted foyer facing a low counter. To her left were several rows of chairs. Beyond these, and separated from them by a low partition, was a great bare expanse on which individuals and couples were revolving, with apparent ease and considerable speed, in a huge circle. As Joshua had said, they were propelled by wheels on their footwear. It was from this area that the sounds of music came, though Ana could not see the players or singers. The whole scene was illuminated by magic lights which, unlike those she had already seen, kept changing hue and seemed to move as well, creating a beautiful pattern of shifting, colored light over the whole spectacle. Her expression must have reflected her delighted wonder, for Joshua, meeting her gaze, smiled broadly.

"Let's get our skates." Leading the way to the counter, he addressed the fat, ferret-faced man behind it. "One ticket, and we'll need two pairs of skates," he said, placing some paper currency on the counter. "I wear a size ten, and I'd say the lady wears a nine or so."

"Well, we don't get much call for women's sizes that big, but I'll see what I can do," was the reply. After putting the paper Joshua had given him in an odd-shaped, ringing container like the one in the general store, and returning some coins that looked as dubious as the ones Ana had received there, the man rummaged on some shelves behind him. "Okay, these oughtta fit. You two have a nice evening."

"Thanks." Taking the two pairs of skates, Joshua led Ana to the nearest empty chairs. "Here," he said, handing one pair to her. "We'll leave our shoes in those shelves there until it's time to go."

Ana began to unlace her brogans, while watching the action on the floor. As she stared, a youth at the far side lost his balance on a turn and landed in an unexpected sitting position. He was up again quickly, skating swiftly sideways to avoid a collision with a couple coming up rapidly behind him. "Doth that happen oft?" she asked Joshua with a wry smile.

He grinned in response. "Not as often as you might think. If you do fall." he added more seriously, "the trick is to just go limp, so you don't have any tension in your body when you land. That way you won't hurt yourself. Then get right up and go at it again. I reckon you'd better hang onto my arm 'til you get used to the wheels."

Accepting this offered support with a murmured thanks, Ana rose and tried a couple of cautious steps. The slipperiness of the skates, and the feel of their weight on her feet, were new and at first disconcerting.

"Don't raise your feet like you do when you're walking," Joshua advised. "Just slide them in the direction you want to go, one at a time, and put your weight on that one." Guided by him to the skating floor, she slipped and slid some at first, but her grip on his arm kept her from falling, and she soon began to gain some control over her own movements and direction.

Joshua was quick to notice her progress. "You're already doing better than I did my first time out," he encouraged. "My feet kept going in separate directions. Before long, you'll be skating better than anyone else here."

To Ana's delight, this prediction was soon fulfilled. After a few circuits of the floor under Joshua's skillful guidance, she found her own instinctive balance and grace coming to the fore. Skating, she discovered, could be as easy as walking, but vastly more exhilarating in its speed and freedom of movement. As they whirled over the floor, the music was sometimes loud and pulsating and the lights flashing and vivid; at alternating times, the rhythm was soft and plaintive and the lights dim and pastel, making it seem as if the gyrating couples were dancing together. Ana lost track of time, and was unaware of the many admiring glances darted at the striking couple. For a time, all she sensed was her own pleasure in the activity and in Joshua's partnership in it, arm in arm with her.

When the roller rink's fat proprietor announced that it was closing time, Ana was reluctant to leave, though she knew she must. "Methinks it cannot be very late, after all," she said wistfully as they were lacing on their own footgear again.

"It's eleven o'clock," Joshua replied, glancing at his watch. "I didn't realize it was that late either." By the time they returned their skates to the counter, the building had largely emptied, and few vehicles were left in the graveled lot when they emerged.

Ana sensed that Joshua was as reluctant as she for the evening to end. Hand in hand under the stars and white-hued moon, they strolled slowly to the waiting vehicle. Neither spoke until they were seated inside. Joshua took his keys from his pocket, but made no move to insert the key into the keyhole.

"Thank you so much for this evening, Joshua," Ana said softly, speaking as warmly as she felt. "I tell you truly, I have ne'er enjoyed myself so greatly as did I these past few hours."

His blush was visible in the unnatural glare of the strange lights along the road, and he gestured disparagingly. "Oh, come on, Ana. As attractive as you are, you've probably had lots of enjoyable dates."

She looked at him quizzically. "There be rich folk in my country who eat dates, Joshua, that come in trade from the lands of the Turks, but never have I tasted any," she said simply.

He stared for a moment, then grinned suddenly. "No, Ana, I didn't mean those kind of dates. In this country, that word has two meanings. I meant, you must have had lots of young men who wanted to enjoy your company."

"In sooth, none!" she exclaimed. She lowered her gaze, then looked up again as Joshua touched her shoulder fleetingly, almost timidly. Their faces were inches apart. Joshua's grey eyes looked into hers, speaking silently of caring and longing, and she knew what message her own eyes sent, whether she willed it or not. Before she could speak again, Joshua leaned forward and paused a moment, still searching her eyes. When she didn't back away, his lips firmly but tenderly met hers in the first kiss she had ever felt (for Miklos' idea of a "kiss" had been strictly teeth to flesh, never lip to lip.)

Before Ana could sort out the confused torrent of emotions—desire and fear, caring and guilt, joy and sorrow—that seemed about to drown her, she felt Joshua draw back and gasp. She opened her eyes and instinctively followed his gaze, then gasped herself as she realized what she had forgotten was directly in front of them. As their two pairs of eyes stared, thunderstruck, side by side into the mirror's surface, only Joshua's stunned eyes stared back.

Chapter Eighteen

How long he stared at the glass surface before him, Joshua did not know. With his entire perception of the nature of reality stood on its head in the space of an eyeblink, such things as time and the world around him no longer mattered. He and Ana might as well have been alone on an otherwise lifeless planet. One phrase echoed and re-echoed in his numbed mind, a phrase from the encyclopedia he'd consulted in the library: "...not casting a reflection in a mirror..." In a blinding instant, the meaning of all the strange circumstances and coincidences that surrounded Ana and her sudden arrival had all become as clear as a landscape lit up by lightning. Obvious unreality had become actual reality; what he had previously dismissed as insane delusion was sober truth. Turning his head slowly, he met Ana's stricken eyes.

"Until now," he whispered in an awed tone, "I never would have believed such a thing could be. I don't know if I believe it now."

"Believe it," Ana whispered dully. The look on her face was like that of a person suddenly lashed with a whip. Her lip trembled slightly, and he saw the moisture begin to fill her widened, dark eyes and start slowly from the corners of each. Without another thought, he opened his arms to her. In another moment, she was leaning her shaking body against his, her arms clasping him as a drowning person might clasp support, and her head finding a resting place on his shoulder as her tears wet his shirt.

"Cry it out," he murmured comfortingly. He did not speak again until her tears had been succeeded by uncontrollable dry sobs wrenching their way up from deep within her, and until these too had finally spent themselves, but his mind was racing all the while. One thing he knew. Reality might be vastly stranger and more complex than he had ever imagined, and there was obviously much about the nature of Ana's being that he didn't understand, but "vampire" or not, the person in his arms was just that: a person, not a monster to be feared. He had read Ana's soul day by day in her eyes and words. The heart beating next to his, he knew, held no malice, and the mouth resting an inch or so from his neck might contain fangs, but not danger.

When she had quieted, and raised herself to face him again, he gently raised one hand and brushed some of the wetness from her face. She reached up and took that hand in hers. "Anyone else would have fled from me, screaming for the whole world to come hither and slay me, Joshua," she said quietly. "It meaneth more to me than I can say that...thee did not."

"I could never run from you, and I'd fight anybody that wanted to hurt you," he said simply. "Ana, you and I have to have a long talk. When...when Jigger ran into the back of that armored car the other night, you were inside it, weren't you?"

Ana nodded. "When that happened, then was the stake that had been put through my heart knocked from my ribs, and I—became again as you see me now. I knew not where I was or how I came to be there. I thought of naught but fleeing away."

"And you turned yourself into a bat to do that?" Joshua said, remembering Jigger's drunken words. "You can do that?" he couldn't resist adding incredulously when she nodded again.

"Yea, canst, and into the semblance of a wolf, or a cloud of mist also, if so be that I will. I do not do it often."

Joshua whistled softly, wondering if he were dreaming. "And you killed those three animals that died around here over the last few days, by drinking their blood?" In spite of himself, he shuddered at this image, then felt stabbed by the pain in Ana's eyes. "I'm sorry," he murmured.

"'Tis not something I like to do, Joshua," she answered, her lower lip trembling again, "but my stomach will hold naught else but blood, and needs must I feed to exist."

"Well," he answered thoughtfully, "it wouldn't be anything I'd like to do, either. But when you stop to think of it, the rest of us aren't vegetarians any more than you are. In the movies and horror stories, they always portray vampires attacking people."

Ana shivered visibly. "Some do...I think the Undead are like the living in one way, Joshua, that there be among them differences of mind and heart, and even that they have the same sort of mind and heart they had when they were alive. Some were ever ruthless and cruel, even when they could walk in the sunlight. But Joshua, I swear to you by...by the One I cannot name, I have never drunk from a human throat. I could not...I could not do to another what was done to me." Joshua stared at her, sensing some of the pain behind her words.

"You must have gone through the agonies of hell," he said slowly. "Do you want...would it help to tell me about it?"

"It wouldst, for I have not had anyone to speak of it with, not for a very long time." She took a deep breath, and her eyes took on a faraway look of remembrance. "Know you, then, Joshua, that I was born in the year 1640..."

Joshua listened, occasionally nodding or asking a question, as she related the story of her journey to Brasov and what it had led to, her existence at Castle Trina and how that had ended, and her journey to England and what had befallen her there. Twice he clenched his fists in helpless anger—once when she described what Miklos Trina had done to her in the Bear's Head, and once when she recounted the last moments beneath the chantry.

When she had finished, he looked into her troubled eyes. "Ana, you've said all along that you wanted to go to a big city. That was because you didn't want to be where you could get close to anybody, or let anybody get close to you, for fear that someone would find out...about you, wasn't it?" At her nod, he continued. "Now that I know, does that change? I mean, wouldn't it be better for you to stay here where you have a friend?"

She shook her head, her expression pained. "Nay, Joshua," she said earnestly. "You...you want us to be more than friends, and that cannot be. I am not the sort a mortal man can court. 'Tis better for you—for us both— if I go away. And did I not, how long would it be ere your mother and sister learned what I am, and what wouldst happen then? And how much peril from this varlet Itchy am I putting ye in by staying? Even when he be caught, I canst not bide here; your sheriff would have me testify at his trial. How would you have me explain why I cannot walk into a courtroom by daylight?"

That point, Joshua realized, had escaped his attention. The whole situation was so bizarre and confusing; how could anyone consider it logically! He rubbed his fingers distractedly across his forehead. "But, Ana," he said, "you need someone to help you, to protect you—I know you want to take care of yourself, but remember what happened in England! I'm pretty sure we've seen the last of Itchy. But what he figured out, other people might figure out, too. And what about Dr. Liskowski? She was watching the house Sunday. She must have some idea of following you when she sees you leave it. What if she should see you ...uh...."

"She canst not watch at all times, Joshua. Needs must she sleep at certain seasons, which she will most likely do in the very small hours. 'Tis then that I go out to feed.

I did so on Sunday night," Ana added, "and 'tis plain that she saw me not then."

"But you don't know that she won't decide to change her schedule sometime, just because she guesses that you don't expect her to," Joshua argued, unconvinced.

Ana sighed. "These be better reasons for me to go from hence, and speedily, than to bide here, Joshua," she said.

"Dr. Liskowski might follow you somewhere else, though," he pointed out. "At least here, you've got somebody who.... Listen, when do you need to...feed again?"

"I would fain do so tonight, but I canst wait a night or two."

"For your own safety's sake, I really wish you would stay in the house, where it's safer, 'til you absolutely have to go out." An idea occurred to him. He bit his lip, but kept his voice steady. "Listen, Ana—you don't...drink enough blood at a time to really hurt a person, do you? I mean, people donate blood all the time to the Red Cross."

Ana stared at him. "Be that some manner of blood-letting ceremony at your church?"

"Oh, no, nothing like that. It's a...well, never mind that now. What I mean is, Ana, that if it'll keep you safe and keep you from starving, I—I wouldn't hold back my blood from you. This Janos you spoke of—he didn't die from...giving blood," he added desperately as she shook her head.

"He did not die, but what harm it did to his mind would be a wide question." The light from the distant streetlamp made the sudden moisture in Ana's eyes shine. She brushed her sleeve quickly across her face. "Nay, Joshua, I cannot touch thee that way, but thank thee. And be of good cheer, I shall bide in the house tonight. We shall see what the morrow bringeth, for good or ill." She reached up and gently stroked his cheek once with the tips of her long, taper-like fingers, then lowered her hand into his. "What is, is, and what will be, will be. But if mere wishes could change fate, Joshua, I could wish myself to have been born in thy time and place, strange to me though it be."

"And I wish I had lived in the century you were born in, Ana," he replied, voice hoarse with emotion. "Things would have been a lot different then, for both of us." He let his gaze drop to her hand, thinking fleetingly of the enormous strength it possessed. It lay on his palm as softly as a resting butterfly.

"But things fall out as they must. 'Twere well that you take me back to the old house now, Joshua," she suggested. "There is naught more that can be said, and I keep thee from rest that mayhap thou wilt sorely need."

"I doubt if I'll sleep any tonight. But I'll take you back," he said, inserting the key into the ignition. "I'm going to be praying for guidance and help, for both of us."

"Truly, that can do no harm." But from Ana's fatalistic tone, Joshua sensed that she doubted it would do any good, either.

* * * *

Joshua's prediction that he would not sleep that night was borne out. So it was with bleary eyes and weary muscles that he finished prying out the last of the nails that secured the floorboards of the old hatchery to their underlying supports. He had been thankful all day for the solitude of this job, for the chance to be alone to think through the tangle of his thoughts, to busy his hands with routine tasks that demanded no real involvement of his mind. The churning feelings inside him—a Babel of emotions he couldn't sort out—made it impossible for him to imagine making small talk with anyone.

When he'd finally returned home the evening before, after parting with Ana and driving around aimlessly for an hour, he'd gone straight to his room. At breakfast, he knew that his mother and Molly had noticed his quietness and his distracted, monosyllabic replies to their conversation. Pleading the pressure of his deadline on the demolition contract, he'd told them both that he'd probably work late and that they might expect him when they saw him. He'd used the same excuse to skip lunch and work through when Wade had called to him to come and eat with the construction crew. But this day of solitude had not brought any clarity to his confusion, nor any long-range idea of what to do.

A glance at the western sky told him it was almost sunset. Wade's crew had left over an hour ago. Removing what was left of the hatchery's foundation, his experienced eye saw, would take only a short time tomorrow morning. Now, he intended to go straight to the old house to see Ana. He quickly loaded the remaining loose boards, which he intended to salvage, into the back of his pickup, and brushed the dust and splinters from his clothes. Then, on an impulse, before climbing into the cab he turned and crossed the street to the gas station.

"I just want to use your pay phone," he explained to the grease-smeared attendant who looked out at him briefly from the open garage door.

Grace Pettigrew picked up moments after he finished dialing. "Lewis County sheriff's office," she said, her voice sounding as though her mouth was full of the chocolates he knew she usually munched on while reading her Harlequins. He'd often wondered how Grace managed to stay slender.

"Hi, Grace. It's Joshua Davidson," he said. "Can I talk to Tom or Walter? I want to ask if there's any more news about Itchy—if maybe somebody's spotted him in Illinois?"

"Well, there's no news on him as far I know," the dispatcher replied, having swallowed some of her mouth's contents, "and if anything had come in I'd have taken the call. Tom and Walter aren't here to ask, though. They had to answer a call over to Mallard Lake." Mallard Lake, as Joshua knew, was the small town in the northwestern corner of the county. "The priest at the Catholic Church up there reported a break-in. Said somebody stole a solid gold cross off the altar, right in broad daylight. I swear, I don't know what this world's coming to. It's pretty bad when a church building isn't safe. Say, how's your mom these days? I might give her another Amway order—"

Grace's last few sentences didn't register in Joshua's ears. He was standing transfixed, staring at the telephone without seeing it, as the significance of what she had said exploded into his mind like a burst of Fourth of July fireworks. He broke into her words, his tone tight and intense. "Can you get in touch with Tom and Walter?"

"There's a radio in their car."

"Get through to them as fast as you can. Tell them to meet me at the old Rogers place. Itchy'll probably be there, too." Before Grace could reply, he turned and ran for his truck, praying under his breath, the dropped receiver left dangling by its cord.

Chapter Nineteen

When she came abruptly awake, lying in her usual silent blackness, Ana's first sensation was a presentiment of danger, an unusual feeling of foreboding. In the next instant, she was almost blinded by a flood of brilliant light. When her eyes adjusted to it, she found herself looking straight into the heinously grinning face of Itchy Bruggenhorst, disfigured by several fresh scars. A moment later his hand whipped up, and a foot-high gold crucifix was rammed down against her face and left to lie there.

At the cold touch of the metal, Ana froze. Her immobility was not merely a result of the mind-boggling terror that swept on black wings through her whole being, it was a total physical paralysis for as long as the cross touched her flesh. She could not move foot or hand no matter how much she wanted to flee, nor lips or tongue no matter how much she wanted to scream, nor even her eyes, however sorely she wanted to look away. The prospect of what Itchy was going to do to her did not even enter her mind at first—the stark fear of the object touching her was enough to swallow her whole awareness. But dread of Itchy made itself felt as soon as he spoke.

"Well, just looky who we got here!" he said thickly. "Lady Dracula herself! What's a matter, Toothy? Cat got your tongue? Or can't ya talk with this thing touchin' ya? I knew all along what ya are," he added, his voice rising to a roar. "An' now everybody's gonna know it, everybody that called me nuts because of ya, ya dirty, stinkin' monster!" He struck Ana a gut-wrenching blow in her unprotected belly with the full force of his fist. With some of his fury thus vented, he took a few deep breaths and spoke again in a softer tone, but one laced with a venomous menace that was somehow more frightening than his shouts.

"I got somethin' here to show ya," he said. Into her field of vision, restricted by her immobility and almost totally flat position, he raised a short wooden stake, its sharp, ugly point stained with dirt. "Ya see that, bitch? Sharp, ain't it? I got me this just for you." He touched the point lightly to the corner of her left eye, then, barely touching her flesh and dress, brought it slowly down across her face, neck and chest to rest lightly on the cloth above her left nipple. "I don't think I even need a hammer to ram this baby right square into your boob. I'm gonna make you holler, and bleed outta every hole in your slimy bod, and then I'm gonna watch ya turn into a pile of lousy bare bones, like in the movies. But I ain't gonna do it yet. I wanna watch ya sweat awhile while ya think about it. See, killin' ya's kinda personal with me. It ain't just to shut your mouth, so it's Kay's word against mine. Yeah, I heard all about that little deal on the radio, after I split from the hospital! But there's more to it than that. See, ya kept me from gettin' somethin' I wanted, ya kicked me in the face an' another place that didn't feel very nice, ya made me eat pot an' get sicker'n a dog, ya got me arrested, ya got a rat to chew on me an' put me in the hospital. I couldn't hardly drive a car for the stinkin' bandages! No broad does me like that an' gets away with it." He stopped speaking abruptly and jerked his head up, listening intently as if he thought he heard something. A second later he apparently decided he hadn't, and resumed speaking.

"I thought this all out," he went on, a smug smirk crawling over his ugly face. "I left that car I took by the bridge for the cops to find, so's they'd think what I wanted 'em to think, see, but I swiped another car 'n come back here. "I'd da been here yesterday if I hadn't had to wait to heal up." His countenance darkened in a scowl. "But I'm healed up now, and you're gonna pay—oh, you're gonna pay! An' don't think anybody's gonna come rescue ya, neither! I fixed it so that Jew woman wouldn't be hangin' around here, an' I took this thing," he reached down and ground the crucifix painfully against Ana's flesh for a moment,"from a long ways from here, so's Fuzz-Lip and Barney Fife'd go way out there to sniff around. An' Lover Boy ain't around now, is he? You'n me, we got the whole place to ourselves. An' I got me a good idea of how I can kill some time—'til I kill you!"

Eyes glittering, he dropped the stake and seized Ana's collar with both hands. Jerking both sides of the cloth out from under the crucifix that rested partly on her chest, with a single savage motion, he ripped her dress down the middle.

Nausea trickled through Ana's insides, fed by helpless rage, horror and misery. To realize that she was soon to relive the same nightmarish pain she had felt the first time a stake entered her heart—which to her memory was an event of about a week ago—was awful enough. But to know that the final agony would be preceded by this ultimate violation was almost more than sanity would bear. The sole consoling thought that flickered in her was that her paralysis would deny Itchy the satisfaction of hearing her whimper or cry out. Her tormentor leaned over her, filling her vision with his leering face, and opened his mouth to speak again.

In that instant, Ana heard the cellar door fly open. As Itchy wheeled and straightened, Joshua's voice boomed, "Itchy, stop it! Now!"

A note of almost comic consternation appeared in Itchy's voice. "How'd ya...? Ya ain't been comin' 'til later."

"Give it up now, Itchy," Joshua said, a steely determination in his tone which Ana had never heard before. His footfalls advanced down the cellar steps. "It's over. I don't want to have to hurt you."

"Hurt me? Ya don't wanna hurt me?" Itchy shrieked. "Ya stinkin' nerd, I'm gonna hurt you—I'm gonna kill ya dead with this stake, an' say she done it, ya—" The obscene epithet he added was drowned in the crash as Joshua tackled him.

By now, the almost overpowering relief Ana had felt when Joshua first appeared had been replaced by mortal terror, not for herself, but for him. Helpless, she listened to the sounds of the fierce struggle for what seemed an eternity, though it could not have been more than a few minutes. She could see almost nothing of the fight save whirling, grappling shadows. But she felt herself jostled twice and could hear the sounds of blows and panting, of Itchy cursing, and once of the crash as the electric lantern from upstairs—which, as she'd guessed, Itchy had brought to the cellar—was knocked to the floor. Her desire to leap up to Joshua's aid was so palpable she could taste it. Suddenly, one of the combatants stumbled into her and sent her rolling.

Landing face first against the wall, she realized the crucifix had fallen away behind her. Fear still clung to her like a blanket, but she could move! Yet even as she raised her eyes, what she saw by the glow of the fallen but unbroken lantern tore a scream from the very core of her.

Itchy had broken into a run and nearly gained the top of the stairs. Joshua, taking steps two at a time, was almost at his heels. Before Ana could move, he had jerked his opponent around by the shoulder and swung a powerful punch at his jaw. But in the same instant, Itchy launched a point-first, powerful thrust of his stake squarely at Joshua's unprotected chest. Both blows connected. Ana saw the stake's point erupt in a gush of blood from Joshua's back, then vanish again as Itchy fell sideways and toppled from the unrailed stair. His screech of terror ended suddenly in mid-cry as his head bounced on the dirt floor. Ana barely heard this, her whole attention on Joshua as he turned, supporting himself against the wall, and stumbled down the steps to collapse at the bottom.

In a heartbeat, she was at his side. He lay in a rapidly forming lake of blood, which was pumping from the wound in his chest with great spurts. Beside herself with panic and remorse, she ripped pieces from her already torn dress and held them to the wound in a frantic attempt to contain the bleeding. Blood was all over her in moments—over her hands and arms, her exposed chest, her feet and legs as she knelt in it, even her hair as she tried to keep the dark strands out of her eyes. She felt very strange inside. She wondered if she were going to faint. To her horror, she saw her efforts failing; the bleeding could not be stopped.

Did she hear footsteps? Joshua opened his eyes and saw her, whispered something she couldn't hear, then closed his lids again. "Joshua!" she screamed fruitlessly.

A hand touched her shoulder. Turning slightly, she saw Tom Saddler kneeling beside her. "I'll take over here," he said firmly. "Walter," he barked at another man Ana barely glanced at, "call the ambulance!" His gaze swiftly took in Ana's ripped dress, and the crucifix and bloody stake on the floor, the latter lying next to Itchy's still form. "Doc, do what you can for this lady, please."

"Of course," Leah Liskowski's voice answered softly. Ana, her eyes widening, turned to see the woman standing behind her. Totally distraught, not knowing what she hoped to accomplish by doing so, Ana forced herself to stand. Her question as to whether or not she was going to faint was abruptly answered. Her legs gave way, and the last thing she knew was that the dirt of the floor was in her face.

*   *   *   *

When consciousness returned, Ana found herself lying on a large padded piece of furniture, shaped like a chair but long enough for her to lie on at full length. The room around her was softly lit and comfortably furnished, with one or two windows that showed the night sky. She was wrapped in a soft blanket. As recent memory came flooding back, she sat up, looking frantically around her. This room was evidently part of a house. Through the open doorway facing her, she could see into the next room as well. Judging by the trivets hanging on its wall, and the teakettle and rack of knives she could see from where she sat, that room must be a kitchen, built into the house as kitchens were in England. At the sound of light footsteps behind her, Ana turned her head and started violently at the sight of Leah Liskowski entering the room through another door.

"Don't be upset, Ana," the scholar woman said quickly. She came forward to sit on a rocking chair beside Ana, regarding her with an intent but not hostile expression. "Are you feeling a bit steadier than you were earlier?"

"What happened? Where is Joshua?" Ana demanded, ignoring the woman's question.

"You fainted, and Joshua is at the University of Iowa Hospital in Iowa City," was the reply. "And young Mr.

Bruggenhorst is dead, by the way. He didn't survive his fall in the cellar. This is Joshua's home. Both the Davidson ladies are at the hospital with him, but they offered to open their home to you under the circumstances, especially since the family they were sheltering were able to leave earlier this evening. I offered to stay with you, and to make some phone calls to the rest of their family."

"Is Joshua going to be all right?" The question was asked with desperate intensity.

Leah took a deep breath, but met Ana's gaze as she answered. "It doesn't look very good for him," she said simply. "He is—or was, at last report—still unconscious, and I'm told his heartbeat and breathing had stopped when the ambulance arrived." As Ana brought her hand up to her mouth to keep from crying out, Leah added quietly, "Please don't assume the worst yet, Ana. Modern medicine can do a great deal more than physicians in your time could." It took a second or two for the full import of the words to register in Ana's mind.

She straightened, staring. "I-I don't know what you mean." Her eyes widened with fear as the human female reached down for the shoulder bag that rested against the chair.

Seeing this, Leah smiled faintly. "I left my crucifix in my car, Ana; you needn't be afraid on that score. All I'm reaching for is this," she added, taking out a folded paper. "As I said, I had followed newspaper accounts of the museum exhibit that was burnt up. The vampire skeleton was abnormal in the size of the canine teeth, but it was unusual in another way—which only a couple of the longer stories mentioned in passing. Namely, that it had belonged to a female in her early twenties who was six feet tall. Not many females of any era are that tall. And this morning, I received this fax from Romania. It seems that the only Ana Vasilifata born in Nagy Timpa was baptized in 1640. After that, she disappears from the church records. For some time, I resisted the obvious conclusion, because it's so fantastic. But it certainly explains some of the recent events, and the perplexing physical evidence at the accident scene. And Mr. Ficklin's claim to have seen a bat fly away from the scene." She paused. "He really did see that, didn't he?"

"Are you not afraid, Leah Liskowski," Ana asked slowly, after another pregnant pause, "to sit here in an empty house face-to-face with one of the Undead?"

Leah merely shrugged. "Should I be?" she replied calmly.

Ana slumped back against the cushions and shook her head, feeling a great weariness of spirit, more heavy than any weariness the body alone could know. "Nay, no mortal need fear me. And what of you? If I would continue to exist, need I fear you?"

Now it was the other who shook her head emphatically. "You might have needed to, if you had attacked human beings in the last few days. But I realized that you fed on animals because you choose not to do so on people. Your...your kind, Ana, are a...a life-form nobody knows much about, and as a scientist what I do is to try to learn about the unknown, not to fear and destroy it. Nor necessarily to judge it, either." She looked at Ana with frank curiosity. "You can teach me much, Ana.

Your existence is the most revolutionary discovery in the field of parapsychology since it began."

Ana quirked one eyebrow in spite of herself. "And you came in haste to make sure your claim to that discovery?" she said dryly.

"Actually, I came as hastily as I did because I thought the late Mr. Bruggenhorst might be going to try something nasty. I'd had to drive up to Dubuque this morning to see a former student of mine whose fax machine I'd arranged to use to contact the Romanian authorities, and I didn't get back 'til evening. When I did, I found a note taped to my motel room door, complete with misspelled words and punctuation errors, telling me to come to a cemetery in Illinois for information about the vampire. It didn't take me long to guess who'd scrawled the note, or why he wanted me in the opposite direction from the old house where you were staying. The sheriff's department dispatcher told me Mr. Saddler and his deputy were already en route, and I met them there a few minutes later; we pulled up at the same time."

Not all the details of this recital had been clear to Ana, but the gist of it was. She dropped her eyes, abashed. Her glance fell on a framed picture of a group of people—Joshua, Molly, their mother, and some others she guessed were the other siblings of the family—on the low table between her and Leah. Even as preoccupied as she was, she noticed the picture's remarkable detail; the painter had been incredibly gifted. "I owe you an apology for my words, just now, and my thanks as well, Doctor." She then noticed a basin of reddish-colored water on the table, with a wet cloth lying in it.

"You may as well call me Leah. I didn't want to ruin the Davidson's couch, so I put some trash can liners under you and took the liberty of cleaning you up a bit," she explained. "I hope you don't mind."

"Nay, I thank you, Leah. You have been kinder to me than I have any right to expect."

"Well, then, suppose you slip on this pair of pajamas from upstairs, while I go out to the kitchen and brew myself a good big pot of strong coffee. And then, when I come back, will you tell me everything about yourself, and let me ask you some questions? And we need to make some plans, too, about where we go from here with what we know—especially since Sheriff Saddler is planning to come by tomorrow morning to take your statement, and he's going to have to be given some explanation as to why that can't happen."

Ana stroked her chin thoughtfully for a second, then looked up again. "Aye, be it so, Leah. I owe you the knowledge you seek, at any rate. So when you return, you may hearken to all you wish to know."

* * * *

"...And the rest of my tale be known to you already," Ana finished hours later. Glancing up, she saw that her companion had finally fallen asleep in the chair, her glasses slightly askew, the instrument she called a "tape recorder' still humming on the table.

Ana rose gracefully, looking down at Leah's peaceful expression and the rhythmic rise and fall of the sleeping woman's bosom as she snored softly. *Were you alone in a room like this with Miklos, or Maria*, she thought, *it would not behoove you to sleep so unafraid.* Her brow furrowed reflectively. Had they really been, in life, as savagely cruel as they were when she had known them? Or had they begun their existence among the Undead with a heart and a conscience not unlike her own, which slowly died inside them after years of emptiness and fear and loneliness? And if that were true, what might she be like after centuries of the same? It was better for things to be as she had already decided they would. She had put off Leah's attempts to talk about tomorrow, knowing what she would do, and knowing, too, that the doctor would object.

Quietly, she rose, picked up the framed picture of Joshua and his family, and stood for a moment looking at his image, as her eyes slowly filled. Leah had said that his heartbeat and breath had stopped, and that meant only one thing. And whether or not physicians now were more skilled than those of her day, she knew they could not bring life back into the dead.

It was my fault, she told herself. It happened because of me, because I came here, because I exist. In her heart, she knew that had they met centuries ago at the Maiden's Fair, she would have come down from Gaina Mountain as Joshua's betrothed. She would have become his wife and found the fullness of her own happiness in making him happy. Now, with no reward, he had laid down his life—a life as much more worthy than hers as gold was more precious than garden dirt—to save her from harm. His death was on her hands, on her conscience, just as surely as his shed blood had been on her person.

Raising the picture to her lips, she kissed the glass over Joshua's likeness, then carefully replaced it on the table. In another moment she had turned and, stepping lightly, walked to the kitchen doorway. It took only a few seconds to find and unlock the back door of the house, which led to a roofed porch. The porch boards felt cool against her bare feet, for Leah had removed the blood-soaked shoes Ana had been wearing when she'd fainted, and there had seemed no point in putting them back on. Lifting her glance above the alley and the backs of the houses on the other side, she scanned the eastern sky. Sunrise was not far off. Her heart raced and her mouth felt terribly dry, but there was no faltering of her resolve. As Joshua's spirit had passed out of this world that night, so her own would pass in a few moments. The world, made poorer by his going, would be benefited by hers. That the two would meet beyond this world, she did not dare hope; she had no prospect of going where Joshua was now. But at least she would end an interminable existence that now added to its miseries the unspeakable desolation of his absence. And she would vanish quickly and cleanly, probably painlessly, or with no more than an eyeblink of pain. She would not expire in slow agony, as Maria had.

Minute by minute, the sky was lightening. For one last time, she let herself look at the simple beauty of the world she was leaving—the green grass and trees, the varicolored flowers, the pale whiteness of the waning moon, low in the sky and framed by wispy clouds. As she took a deep, calming breath, the morning breeze brought to her nostrils a last sweet scent of lilacs. Then she shut her eyes, trembling a little, and waited.

Werner Lind

Chapter Twenty

Wakefulness returned to Joshua gradually. At first, he was aware only that he was lying in the dark and that strange, colored lights seemed to be dancing around in his head. These slowly faded, and he sensed that it seemed dark because his eyes were still closed. But as yet, he hadn't mustered the energy to open them. He began to be dimly aware of a dull ache in his chest, and of a lesser discomfort in his left arm.

Memory suddenly exploded into his mind, and he opened his eyes abruptly. He promptly closed them again, almost blinded by the light which greeted him. When he had better prepared himself, he cautiously raised his lids again, revealing the welcome sight of his mother's tear-streaked but smiling face. Responding to a soft touch on his right arm, he turned his head slightly to that side of the bed to see Molly, her grin a picture of delight.

"Is Ana all right?" he said immediately, his voice hoarse and weak-sounding to his own ears.

Molly's grin widened. "Mom, didn't I bet you the first thing he'd say would be exactly that? I guess she is—she fainted when you got hurt, and Leah took her to our place to stay. We haven't had a chance to talk to Ana since, and we just talked to Leah for a minute to let her know you were going to be okay. Itchy's not okay, though. He busted his neck falling down the cellar stairs, and he was D.O.A. at the emergency room. So he won't be bothering you, or Ana, or anybody else, ever again."

Joshua stared at her a moment as he absorbed this information. "I...I didn't mean to kill him," he said slowly. "Although he sure meant to kill me."

"He almost did," Mary Davidson said in a breaking voice. "Oh, son, we thought for sure we had lost you! You lost so much blood, and it took sixty-seven stitches inside and out to close your wound, and they said you were clinically dead. Oh, Joshua, we prayed; we all prayed so hard..." Her voice failed and she clutched his hand. He would have raised it to her cheek, had he not already discovered that he had an IV connected to that arm. By now, he was also aware of some metallic objects he couldn't see attached to his head, and apparently connected to something behind him which he couldn't see either.

"It's all right, Mom," he said, as reassuringly as he could. "If I were going to die, I'd have to feel a lot worse than I do now. I'll be around to bug you for quite a while yet, I reckon."

"Oh, we've known that for hours," Molly said, "ever since the EEG showed your higher brain waves coming back on at about five o'clock this morning. The doctors here didn't know what to make of it—they still don't. I told them it was God's answer to our prayers, but they just laughed. But anyway, they got Dr. O'Riordan on the phone—"

"Wait a minute," Joshua said. "Where am I? This isn't Lewis County Hospital?"

Molly shook her head. "No, this is Iowa City. Anyway, he said you'd come around when you were ready, and that then they could give you some juice to see if you can take it, and that he'll be out here this afternoon when he finishes his rounds back home. And he said they should let us sit with you. I don't think they were too crazy about that idea. I think they only let us because I'm a nurse, and they said it could only be the two of us in here with you, nobody else. I expect they'll chase us out soon. When you opened your eyes the first time I buzzed the nurses' station and told them you were starting to wake up—"

"Yes, and now I need to examine him," said an unfamiliar voice from the doorway. Joshua looked over to see a thick-set, chubby-cheeked man of about thirty-five, with fair hair and thick glasses. His white gown and stethoscope identified him as a doctor. "I'd appreciate it if you ladies would wait back in the visitor's lounge."

"Of course," Mrs. Davidson replied. She bent and kissed her son's forehead. "We'll see you later, dear." Molly gave his shoulder an affectionate squeeze, then followed her mother out.

The physician came forward to the bed, regarding Joshua with open interest. "Good morning, Mr. Davidson! I'm Dr. Richardson, one of the residents here.

I really never expected to be introducing myself to you."
He put the ends of his stethoscope into his ears.

Joshua raised his eyebrows. "Was I really in that bad
a shape, Doctor?"

"Frankly, yes. That stake you were stabbed with
missed your heart, but it went clean through your left
lung, and you lost so much blood that it sent your brain
into shock. I need you to breathe deeply for me. Ah, yes,
good. And again. And once again. Very good. There's no
fluid at all in your lungs. That could have been a problem
with this type of wound, but it doesn't appear that it will
be." From his pocket, he took a device that looked like a
Magic Marker with a lens instead of a point. "Now, I
need you to follow the beam of light with your eyes as I
move it... yes, like that. Excellent."

"What does that tell you?"

"That you still have the ability to focus and move
your eyes. If you couldn't, it would be an indication of
brain damage. But there's no such indication. Most
remarkable. In all candor," he added, pushing the nurse's
call button and taking a small rubber-headed hammer
from his other pocket, "I believed you would always
remain a comatose vegetable. The paramedics restarted
your heart on the way over here, and we were finally able
to wean you from the respirator, but I really considered
the IV a waste of resources." He paused to throw back
the blanket and tap Joshua's knees and elbows with the
hammer, nodding and beaming at the jerks this elicited.
"But your family and your hometown doctor insisted on
it, so we decided to humor them, especially since you had
signed an advance directive that required us to. It's a

good thing we did. I don't mind admitting, your recovery makes me feel a bit sheepish."

"Why?" Joshua said dryly. "Just because you wanted to starve and dehydrate me after I'd been here only a few hours?"

"A few hours?" Dr. Richardson repeated, staring. "Oh, they didn't tell you. No, you were comatose for about three days and nights, Mr. Davidson. This is Sunday morning." As wide-eyed surprise washed over Joshua, a young nurse appeared in the doorway. "Nurse, tell the kitchen that this patient can have some juice, as per his own doctor's instructions. We'll see how he does with it."

"Yes, Doctor. Oh, and one of the ladies—not one of the two who were in here, another one who just came—is asking if she can come in." Tess, the younger of his two sisters, must be here too, Joshua realized. Evidently she had been summoned from Wisconsin. He wondered if her husband Jordan had come with her.

"I don't see why not. And I believe the sheriff from Lewis County plans to come later this morning to take a statement. He may come in, too, but I don't want more than two visitors in the room at a time. It's best not to tire Mr. Davidson out." He bent to examine the readings on the monitors behind Joshua.

As the patient listened to the nurse's receding footsteps, a sudden thought came to him. "Today's Easter Sunday," he murmured, almost to himself.

"What? Oh, yes, Easter, of course. The day for all the kiddies to pig out on Easter candy. I know mine'll be up to their little ears in jelly beans and chocolate bunnies.

But, it only comes once a year, right? Now, we'll want to see whether or not you keep the juice down, and we'll check on this EEG from time to time over the next few days, but I don't expect any problem. Your brain waves are normal, your reflexes are perfect, and your wound isn't draining, which indicates that it's healing without infection. At this point, my prognosis is for a full recovery, and I expect your Dr. O'Riordan will agree with me. I'll see you later this morning."

"Thank you, Doctor," Joshua replied politely. Knowing where thanks were really due, he bowed his head in a short but heartfelt prayer, adding petitions for Ana's safety to gratitude for his own recovery. Unease about her welfare was the one disturbance of his peace of mind right now; he wasn't sure he liked the idea of her being alone with a parapsychologist who suspected too much. Then his eye fell on a few get well cards on the bedside table, and he began to read the inscriptions and signatures of various individuals and couples from the Zion congregation.

Hearing the sound of someone in the doorway, he looked up to greet his sister. He caught his breath, staring incredulously at something that could not possibly be. Framed in the doorway, wearing jeans and a dark blue blouse, and her long black hair secured by a plastic headband, stood Ana! In the strong sunlight that fell full on her from the window, he could see the glint of happy tears in her eyes. Her face beamed with a radiant joy he had never seen on it before, and looking closely, he saw something else he had never before noticed—a hint of coloring in her complexion. Her usual pallor, he realized, was simply not there.

"How...?" he said, holding out his hand to her as joy and amazement surged through him like whitewater breakers through a canyon.

Ana came forward and caught his hand in her own, seating herself beside him on the edge of the bed. "'Twas thy blood, Joshua," she answered, in a voice husky with emotion. "'Twas thy blood which freed me from my curse."

Joshua stared at her, his brow furrowing with perplexity. "I...I don't understand how—"

"Nor do I, in full. Nor does Leah Liskowski, though 'tis she who guessed that the key did lie in that. She says that blood was taken from me for to make me what I was, and that...that thy blood had healing power in somewise, not merely because 'twas blood, but because thee let it be shed for me out of...out of..." She paused, blushing becomingly for the first time since Joshua had met her.

Squeezing her hand tightly, he finished the sentence for her. "Out of love?"

Silently, she nodded. Holding hands, the two stared wordlessly into each other's eyes for a few moments, awed and thankful for the great and wondrous mystery that had taken place.

Dropping his gaze, he observed for the first time the thin silver necklace Ana was wearing, from which hung a tiny cross. "Before now, I couldn't have imagined you wearing a necklace like that."

Ana touched the cross lightly with a fingertip. "'Twas Leah's gift to me just now, after bringing me hither, ere she returned to her home. Though she be a Jewess, she uses such like things in studying folk who believe themselves to be Undead. But she said she couldst get another, and that she believed 'twould mean much to me. And she believed truly. For long, I could not wear this sign. Now I would wear it always upon my neck, but more—I would wear it always within my heart."

As she finished speaking, a knock on the open door of the room startled them both. Turning his head, Joshua looked into the unusually serious, almost grim, face of Tom Saddler. "Come on in, Tom," he said quietly. "It's good to see you."

"Mornin', Josh, and good mornin' to you, Ana. It's good to see you again, too, buddy. There was a time I thought I wouldn't. I wish I wasn't comin' here on official business, but the fact is, I have to get statements from both of you." He paused to sink into the chair Joshua indicated and to fidget briefly with the pencil and yellow legal pad he carried, then went on. "I'm especially interested in gettin' a statement from you, Ana, since you've been avoidin' me for the past three days. And I got somethin' in the mail yesterday, in response to an inquiry I sent to Washington, which I'm afraid raises quite a few questions. It seems the government's got no record of an Ana Vasilifata enterin' this country legally." He fixed a stern gaze on her. "Somethin' mighty fishy's been goin' down here, and you're goin' to tell me all about it, and you're goin' to tell me right now. Do you understand that?"

Ana nodded, facing the sheriff with an outward calmness belied only by the slight trembling of her hands. "Aye, I do understand, and I shall tell you all you wish to know, right willingly. I wouldst have ere now, but that Leah counseled me to wait." She held up a hand to forestall Tom's angry interjection. "For she said you shouldst deem me mad and lock me up, unless Joshua couldst confirm what I have to tell. And wilt thou bear me witness, Joshua? I know not what will befall me, but whatever it be, I would speak truth at last, and have no more of dark secrets to hide," she added earnestly.

Joshua nodded. "You're right, Ana. The truth is what we have to tell."

Tom raised his brows, then knit them. "Maybe you two had better begin at the beginin'."

Ana cleared her throat and sat up straighter. "Yea, that would we," she began, the tremor in her voice barely detectable. "'Tis a long tale, in sooth, and it begins long ago, in Transylvania, where I was born..."

While Ana and Joshua, speaking alternately, shared the young woman's whole story—interrupted only briefly by the entry of a nurse's aide with Joshua's juice, which he drank perfunctorily without tasting—Tom sat silent. First he wore an expression of puzzlement, then of disbelief, and finally of awed wonder. A few times he opened his mouth as if to interrupt but restrained himself and motioned them to continue. When they had finished, he continued to sit silently for several long moments, staring first at one and then at the other.

Finally, he spoke slowly. "Josh, that's the biggest bunch of unbelievable nonsense anybody ever told me." He looked his friend squarely in the eye. "And you're tellin' me it's the honest-to-God truth, aren't you?"

Joshua nodded. "Yes, Tom, that's what I'm telling you."

The sheriff sat back in his chair and whistled softly, then turned his gaze to Ana. "If anybody but Josh here told me this stuff, I'd call for the whitecoats to come with a butterfly net. But I know that this man isn't crazy—and I know he doesn't lie. You'll both have to pardon me," he added after a pause, shaking his head as if to clear it. "All this...takes a bit of gettin' used to. All right, now. As sheriff, it's my responsibility to determine whether information presented to me requires any further action. In the light of all the material facts here—a big one bein' that if I do pursue this, all three of us'll have ourselves a new address, over at Mount Pleasant in the state mental hospital—my official judgement is that this information doesn't require further action. No crime's been committed. There's nothin' in the Code of Iowa about vampires, Ana here didn't cause the armored car accident, and the animals that...died, had no owners, so no complaints have been filed. And the coroner's already ruled that Itchy died by misadventure durin' the committin' of an attempted felony, and nothin' either one of you said this mornin' changes that one bit. You wanted to do the right thing by tellin' me the truth, and you told me, and I respect you for it. I'm officially tellin' you that the right thing to do now is to drop the whole matter—just call it a classified sheriff's department secret, okay?"

Joshua extended his hand and clasped the sheriff's warmly. "You won't hear any argument out of us. Thanks, Tom."

"Don't mention it—to anybody!" Tom added with a grin. "I'm sure not goin' to." He turned slightly and took the hand that Ana impulsively offered, looking at her with frank amazement. "You've sure been through some things I never would have thought could happen in real life, Ana, but if you had to go through 'em, I'm glad they turned out as well as they have. It's kind of late to say it, but welcome to America—and to the twenty-first century."

"Thank you, Tom—for everything."

"Now," he said briskly, "I'll leave you two alone, 'cause I want to talk to that sister of yours a bit before I go, Josh."

"Keep her straight, Tom. We'll see you again soon, I hope." With a wink and a wave, the sheriff departed, closing the door behind him.

As Joshua and Ana turned to look at each other, Joshua knew that the happiness and relief on her face was mirrored on his own.

"I-I have been given another life," she said softly, the strength of her emotion evident in her tone. "And now the chance to live that life in peace, without being made a freak for all the world to use as a gazingstock."

Something Ana had said earlier came back to Joshua's mind. "You said Leah knows what you were. Will she keep your past to herself?"

Ana nodded. "Aye, for she said I was owed that, and that moreover she had no proof of what she had found, leastways none that folk would believe. But she is minded to go again to Transylvania come summer. She says that now that she knows the Undead truly exist, she means to prove it to all the world—and belike she will someday. I fear not for her safety. She be brave and clever enough to handle aught that may come her way, I'll warrant."

Joshua rubbed his chin thoughtfully. "And what about you, Ana? I know Transylvania is your home; will—will you be going back there now?"

She paused a moment, considering her words. "The Transylvania of this day be not my home, Joshua. All the people and things that I knew are gone to dust long ago, and I have naught more there than in any other place."

"Then, Ana," he said, "I-I want you to know that you have something here. I mean, that you have a home here; if you want it, that is..." A blush hot on his face, his hand sought and found hers on the blanket. He felt unimaginably awkward and tongue-tied, and was certain that he wasn't expressing himself well at all. But from the expression in Ana's eyes as they looked into his, that didn't seem to matter.

"Aye, I want it," she said simply. "More than anything in this world." As he opened his mouth to speak again, she raised her free hand to gently touch his lips with the ends of her long fingers. "What is in thy heart to say, Joshua, thou hast said already with more and better than words. But the words will be said when thou art well and strong again, and to hear them will be sweeter than honey in my ears—and in my heart as well."

Answering her smile with his own, Joshua warmly kissed the fingers that touched his lips. Looking down at their firmly clasped hands, he knew that his heart and the heart of this exceptional woman sent to him across the centuries would be joined just as firmly, as long as both continued to beat. And the knowledge was as bright and glorious as the sunlight that streamed over them both.

Werner Lind

About the Author

Werner A. Lind was born in Minneapolis, but raised in eastern Iowa. A graduate of Clinton (Iowa) Community College and of Bethel College in North Newton, Kansas, he also holds master's degrees from Eastern Mennonite Univ. in Harrisonburg, Virginia and from Indiana State Univ. Formerly a college teacher and a public librarian, he and his wife Barb now live in Bluefield, Virginia, where he has been a librarian at Bluefield College since 1992. They have three daughters. His short fiction, book reviews and scholarly articles have been published in various periodicals and online, and he has twice won prizes for his work in fiction. *Lifeblood* is his first novel.

www.ingramcontent.com/pod-product-compliance
Lightning Source LLC
Chambersburg PA
CBHW050038180626
46810CB00002B/781